THE SUNKEN CITY

ISBN: 978-1-957121-36-9

Text © 2023 by Tim Curran

Cover Artwork © 2023, by K. L. Turner

Interior and cover design by Cyrusfiction Productions

Editor and Publisher, Joe Morey

Weird House Press
Central Point, OR 97502
www.weirdhousepress.com

THE SUNKEN CITY

TIM CURRAN

WEIRD HOUSE

1
KHARKOV STATION

Kharkov still stood.

Alone and silent and grim, it still stood.

Despite many harsh winters that had elapsed since the tragedy, it had not fallen or been eroded away by the ice-winds. It waited, a collection of orange-striped metal buildings—the boxy slab of the power station, the oval meteorology dome, the rising bubble of the observatory, the long and low rectangle of Targa House capped by aerials and antennas, and the numerous garages and outbuildings and huts beyond.

They had stood silent and empty for years, prey to ice and snow and the unbearable cold that blew in across the polar plateau, the bitter weather that swept down from the jagged promontories of the Dominion Range. Like monuments to something long dead, they waited and watched.

The station had seen tragedy and horror and nightmare given flesh. And no structure, regardless of how sterile and lifeless, could absorb that much malefic energy without holding some of it in its dark belly, a palpable miasma that oozed from the walls and ceilings, an evil that dripped thickly from every rivet and plank and joist.

And if you were alone there for any length of time, you would have felt these things, knew these things, for they would have flooded you and poisoned you, devoured you joint by joint, filling your head with blank echoing screams and the profane melodies of things dead for uncounted eons.

For at Kharkov Station, you were never truly alone. Always behind you or out of the corner of your eye, fantastic shapes mocked and whispered. Loathsome memories rustled and crawled.

The summer before, resurrection of a sort had been attempted.

Targa House was cleaned and repaired, the power station refitted, and the old drill Tower which had been bulldozed down by a man name Jimmy Hayes was rebuilt, bigger and grander than ever before. A specially designed thermal drill was brought in that could open up a massive shaft to Lake Vordog, a sub-glacial lake nearly a mile below the ice cap. But those that came in to do the work were grateful when they could leave. They had heard things and seen things at the station, dreaming of that ebon, ancient lake far below and what lived there.

Nobody came right out and said the station was haunted, but they looked upon it as a living thing tormented by its own twisted memories and nightmares, something driven mad by what it had known and would still know.

So, although it had never really been empty and was no longer sane, Kharkov still stood.

2
DIRTY LITTLE SECRETS

While the wind screamed in a bleak voice and shook the compound, the team gathered in the old galley at Targa House and listened to Orr speak of why they had come and what it was they hoped to accomplish. Only Navy personnel were in on the briefing. The techies that operated the drill platform were not invited. Their job was to open the shaft, keep it open and ice-free, and to monitor the diver's habitat some 900 feet below the surface of the lake itself. It had been assembled down there piecemeal by another group that had been flown in for the job and flown out again.

The team that gathered to listen to Orr were all seasoned divers with years of experience in deep-saturation dives and atmospheric suit descents.

Orr was a Navy rear admiral and he liked to talk.

If you wanted to listen, he'd tell you about his hardhat days as a Navy salvage diver or how he blew out his left ear on a submarine mine or his saturation dives with Hydrolab and Sealab III. But today he wasn't talking about any of that. Today what he was discussing was classified and he'd impressed that upon all of them—Murphy and Hubbs, Javonivic and Bell. They had all signed the Official Secrets Act which promised them that if they talked out of school about what they knew and what they would see, they would not be released from a federal penitentiary until they had long white beards.

No big surprise there.

Bell and the others had signed the OSA before and many times. They were all with the Navy's DSU—Deep Submergence Unit—and the DSSP—Deep Submergence Systems Project—-both of which were hooked up with the Office of Naval Research and the Special Projects Office. And when you swam in the shadowy realms of the ONR and SPO, signing the Secrets Act was pretty much a given.

Bell had been in on countless black bag jobs with the DSU.

He had retrieved nuclear warheads from sunken Russian subs and vials of weapons-grade anthrax spores from a Lebanese freighter a U.S. Navy hunter-killer sub had sunk in the Gulf of Aden (said spores were bound for the New York subway system to be released in aerosol form by agents of the Islamic Jihad). And once, he'd been part of a team that went down to the bottom of the Bering Sea to grab a crashed interplanetary probe that had returned from the orbit of Venus with samples of a life-form from the Venusian upper atmosphere that were considered "biologically unstable and potentially pathogenic."

He had always kept his mouth shut and so had the others or they wouldn't be here.

"All right," Orr said, "now let's get to the meat of this boondoggle."

The lights dimmed and all eyes were on the big screen up on the wall. He punched a key on his laptop and a photograph of a man appeared on the screen. He was thin with a craggy, windburned face and a thick mop of back-swept silver hair that made him look like some emaciated version of Charlie Rich.

"This is Henry Charles Gundry, deceased. Gundry was a Caltech glaciologist who was in charge of Project DeepDrill here at Kharkov some five years ago. He helmed the original team that drilled down to Lake Vordog and released the ATP cryobot into the lake itself," Orr told them.

Project DeepDrill had been a NASA operation. Part of the same overall project called the Kronos Experiment that the Cassini 3 spacecraft was involved in as it mapped Jupiter's Jovian moons and dropped the Callisto probe into the trench south of the Valhalla impact basin: laying the groundwork for one of the most impressive deep space missions NASA had yet undertaken, the exploration of the subsurface oceans of Callisto,

Europa, Ganymede, and Io. A wholescale search for extraterrestrial life that would culminate with the Europa Ice Clipper mission which would release high-tech crybots that would melt through the ice of the moons down to the oceans themselves. The ATP—Active Thermal Probe—cryobots were, essentially, robotic submersibles guided by advanced AI packages that would seek out life in those black depths. Gundry had tested several cryobots before he was given the Lake Vordog job. His cryobot worked perfectly. It melted through the ice from the original drilled borehole and descended into the lake itself.

That much was a scientific feat that NASA applauded.

But what it found down there, locked away beneath the ice for forty-million years, was what had scared the shit out of everyone.

"The following images I'm going to show you are from still photos and images captured from live video feed," Orr said. "They were taken by Gundry's cryo over a mile beneath our feet."

Bell looked over at Murphy and Murphy did a Groucho Marx with his eyebrows to say, *okay, here comes the good stuff, old buddy.* The top secret stuff they'd been denying from day one.

Orr punched a few more keys, a series of images appearing on the screen. Nothing earth-shattering, yet extraordinary all the same. Video of the creatures that lived in the lake down below, things unknown to science and others thought long-extinct: colonies of multi-hued jellies that looked like living bubbles, gigantic crabs and sea scorpions, undulant tube worms, bioluminous fish shaped like basketballs, and an immense albino squid-like creature that pulled away into the darkness. Orr didn't call the latter a sea monster, but it certainly fit the necessary criteria.

He punched another key and somebody gasped.

They were seeing the city.

The vast underwater city that was supposedly built by a pre-human intelligence eons before man dropped out of the trees and lost his prehensile tail.

It was incredible.

The first image showed what seemed to be ruins of some sort—arches and broken domes and leaning spires, an assortment of rising and falling shapes encrusted in marine deposits. The next series of images showed monoliths and obelisks, trench systems and fragmented walls that looked like an incredibly elaborate series of barrow tombs capped by megalithic structures.

Orr kept punching his keys and here was the city itself as seen by Gundry's hydrobot, the free-roaming robotic submersible that the cryobot had released on the bottom. It was impossible to get the entire structure in the frame because it seemed to go on forever and there was no way the hydrobot could have pulled back far enough to pan it and still illuminate it with its lights. So what they saw were portions of it, but enough to stitch the whole nightmare architecture into a common whole. It was an enormous honeycombed labyrinth composed of rectangles and towers and arches and spheres all welded together, intersecting and overlapping. A cyclopean profusion, something that looked like it had grown that way rather than been built, and also something that looked curiously machined and geometrically profuse.

"Jesus H. Christ," Murphy said.

Something about it made Bell's skin crawl and his scalp go tight, filled his mind with drifting phantasms and weird, distorted memories that he could not honestly understand. Flashes and glimpses that told him he had seen this all before, but not how or when.

The city looked very much like something insects would build, barren and harsh and almost militaristic. The way it was honeycombed with holes and passages reminded him of the webby lairs of funnel-web spiders. No beings with hearts or souls would have designed something like this. A hive. A grotesque alien hive that looked very much like some vast biomechanical machine out of H. R. Giger, a terrible organic and mechanistic hybrid that had been rotting and rusting away at the bottom of that ancient lake for millions of years, waiting to be activated.

And that was at the core of the fear that Bell felt looking upon it: that it would suddenly wake up.

Orr killed the images, looking at the pale faces of his divers. "It...ah... seems to have an odd effect on anybody who looks at it. It got me the first time I saw it, people. And I'm not too big of a man to admit it scared the shit out of me and gave me nightmares for a week."

"I think I'm having 'em right now, sir," Hubbs said in all seriousness.

Nobody laughed at that.

They were all feeling it deep inside, as if the image of that monstrosity had dredged up half-remembered phobias from the settled, undisturbed sediment at the very bottom of their souls. Something about it made you see things you should not see and feel things you should not feel. It overwhelmed you with anxieties and night terrors that reached out to you from the very dank cellar of the race.

Orr cleared his throat. "I don't know what you people will see below. I really don't. All I know is that at six sharp tomorrow morning, the four of you are going down there."

BOGIES

O rr didn't bother to mention all the psychobabble claptrap that the Navy psychologists told him could be expected from any human beings that looked upon the city—things like *extreme anxiety responses* and *group psychosocial terrors*. He didn't think he needed to. He respected his people and had hand-picked them for the job. This bunch were the rocks of the DSU, a group known for its iron nerve. No, he didn't need shrinks to tell him what he already knew: that the human race in general had an instinctual fear of those goddamned sunken ruins.

That much was obvious.

He had been there when the Lake Vordog dive project was originally discussed. The spooks from ONI and NSF looked like they'd been ready to piss their pants every time the photos were shown. And he had not blamed them.

"Now," he said, running a hand through his white crewcut, "let's talk about this. You've probably heard the bullshit about ancient cities down here and who supposedly built them. Well, that much is true. They are here. As to who built them…I don't know. I was not briefed on that and if I hear one of you people say the word *alien* in my presence or amongst your selves, you'll need a surgeon to remove my size eleven from your assholes. Got it?"

Everyone nodded.

"Okay. Good. Now, the city below us isn't the only one. Same time Gundry was launching his cryo down here five years back, a paleobiologist by the name of Dr. Robert Gates was operating out of this same facility and running a field camp up in the Dominions. He drilled into a subterranean shaft and, lo and behold, he found the ruins of another city. You maybe heard about that. He was supposed to have found the mummies or remains of the...*individuals* that built the city. Is that true? I don't have the faintest." Orr packed his pipe and lit it. "Okay, now Gundry thought that our city below and the one in the mountains might have been part of a common whole at one time and still might be connected by passages beneath the ice cap itself.

"But that's neither here nor there. We're not here as scientists or archaeologists. We're not here to figure out who built that wreck below. We're not concerned about little green men or flying fucking saucers. Our target is that city, plain and simple."

Javonivic raised her hand. "Sir, are we to explore it?"

"No."

"To retrieve something?"

"No."

"Then..."

Orr puffed on his pipe, clouds of smoke rising above his head. "Some six years ago, a magnetic imaging fly-over picked up something that has had the heavy-thinkers scratching their heads ever since: an anomaly. A self-perpetuating magnetic field of incredible intensity and it's centered down there in that city. Background magnetism is, of course, strong down here at the Pole, roughly seventy-thousand nanoteslas in the area of Kharkov, but what's coming out of that city is putting out anything from eighty up to one-fifty with random spikes of two-hundred plus. The field down there fluctuates, but the intensity has been gradually increasing these past five, six years. Currently, it's right off the scale."

The divers looked at each other.

Finally, Bell just went ahead and asked what they were all wondering. "Sir...what the hell could put out that sort of juice? I'm guessing it can't be of natural origin."

"No way. Whatever's down there is artificial and it's getting stronger and stronger. Not much less than a massive electromagnetic power plant could produce the signals we've been picking up."

"And that's our job?" Murphy said. "Enter the city and find that... generator or whatever it is. And then?"

Orr just shook his head. "I have sealed orders. I can't open them until you find that source...then, then we'll see."

Bell didn't say anything.

None of them did. They knew very well what their job would be once that source was discovered. First to document it and then to destroy it. There was no doubt in anyone's mind.

Orr tapped out his pipe in his palm and sat back down at his laptop. "These following images were also taken by Gundry's hydrobot. Pay attention now."

He clicked a key on his laptop and more images appeared on the screen. They were not very distinct. They showed things the forward cameras of the hydrobot had captured: shadows. That's about all they were. On the screen, the hydrobot's lights were filled with rising sediment, glimpses of strange forms swimming in and out of frame. Then more shadows, oblong shapes that darted away from the light before they could be seen. Whatever they were, they were large and weird and very fast, apparently. They moved off before the cameras could get much more than a blurry glimpse.

Orr tapped his keys and they saw still photos of the city again...or part of it. Those oblong shapes were moving in and out of the ruins. Emerging from shafts and holes, slipping into the myriad honeycombed mouths. Again, the shots were indistinct. They could have been anything.

Orr tapped his keys and more images appeared.

And these were the ones nobody wanted to see, for they were absolute vindication of all those half-baked alien stories that had been leaking out of Antarctica for years now.

These images were not blurry.

They were fairly clear.

The oblong forms appeared to be some unknown form of marine life that was cylindrical in shape, wide and barrel-like at midbody, tapering at each end. At the bottom were clusters of thick tentacles that hung limp as they swam. From either side of the body jutted huge fin-like wings that were supported by long and narrow bony rods, smooth flesh webbed in-between, held taut. The bodies were furrowed, a bluish gunmetal gray, more tentacle-like feelers coming from midbody. At the top, there was what looked like more tentacles, but they were short and blunt, rubbery stalks with brilliant red eyes set atop them.

"What the hell are those?" Murphy asked.

But Orr did not answer. What, indeed?

More images showed the things cavorting around the hydrobot, curious maybe. And then the next series showed a veritable swarm of them coming out of the city and crowding the hydrobot's cameras.

That was it.

Orr brought up the lights and everyone seemed to be glad about that.

"Those...those are the things that built the city, aren't they, sir?" Javonivic said, something like raw terror breaking beneath her words. "Those are living representations of the mummies Gates found. The things that the crew at this station were killed by five years ago."

Orr just said, "Yes. Yes, they are."

He explained that there were no more images because when those creatures crowded the hydrobot, transmission ceased. It was assumed they had destroyed it or at least rendered it inoperative.

Nobody said anything for a time. It was a lot to absorb. An awful lot. The sight of those creatures filling the screen had almost been too much. The city was bad enough, but those things...they were like razors scraped over your brain, peeling back some protective layer and cutting into moist pink meat, exposing all the creeping, dark racial memories of humankind and making you know, dear God, *know* that these creatures had inspired just about every one of them. Every nightmare myth and twisted scrap of folklore.

"The Old Ones," Hubbs said in a weak, scratching voice.

The very sound of that name made something curdle and go sour inside of Bell. *The Old Ones, the Old Ones, the Old Ones,* a voice kept saying in his head. And maybe the voice did not need to tell him that, because part of him that had been submerged for what seemed millennia knew those creatures. Somehow. Some way. What they were and possibly what it was they wanted.

Orr sighed. "Yes. Old Ones, Elder Things, Crinoids. But from here on in, they are not to be referred to by any comic book nerd bullshit. They have been designated by the Office of Naval Intelligence as *bogies*. Understood? Good. ONI says bogies, then bogies they are. Okay, these photos are five years old. During the past several months, a DSU engineering team has spent a lot of time below. They have assembled a Neptune-class diver's habitat and platform for us on a plateau some three-quarters of a mile from the outskirts of the city. It was quite a job. The drill team opened up the shaft and widened it. We lowered an ROV and spent ten days finding a suitable location for the habitat. And then, well, our headaches began. Regardless, the Neptune-class structure is down there and it's fully operational."

Orr discussed how the Neptune habitat was put together.

Bell didn't pay much attention to any of that. He knew what kind of job it was. The Neptunes were pre-fab structures. Once the platform was secured, then the sections could be ferried down by submersibles and assembled into a whole like a puzzle. Generally, such an undertaking took two to three weeks, but Lake Vordog had no doubt presented special challenges.

After Orr was done running through his laundry list of engineering details as to how they lowered the equipment and then got it down to the plateau itself, he said, "Like I said, this whole operation went on for months and months, and although there were glitches, the team was never in any danger. They encountered none of these creatures, nor any other dangerous life-form down there. An ROV reconnaissance of the city has not seen any of them either. If they're still there, people, then they're hiding. Beyond that, I cannot say."

But he didn't have to.

Bell could feel them down there, as if he had established some crazy psychic uplink with them as a result of seeing those photos. It made no sense and he knew it. But his mind was a storm of images. The creatures. The city. The city. The creatures. Distorted, aberrant memory and malign association that left him reeling, left him feeling like he was suffocating, as if he could not get enough air and was about to pass out cold.

Something about them, about that city, about all of it was so goddamn familiar. He had no idea why. Only that it was not some fantasy dream-train. It was real. It was solid.

His dread and revulsion of them was absolute and unnerving. He wished to God he had passed this mission up, because the damn thing had been voluntary. Then he would have been safe in blissful ignorance.

But now he had seen them.

And to see them was to know them.

And to know them was to remember them in a hazy, surreal, ephemeral sort of way. One minute, those stark and awful memories were crystal clear, the next muddy and obscure. It was a very transitory thing and all the more frustrating because of which.

He thought: *God, why do I remember that city? Why do I feel like I've seen it before? And why are those Old Ones familiar? I know I've never seen them... but they're in my head like maybe they've always been there. Just waiting for me to make the connection. And now that I have...what happens next?*

Yes, he had never known anything as forbidding as the way all of it made him feel. It was as if merely looking at those horrors had opened up an ancient can of worms in him, worms that were finally free, slithering through him and breeding their looping larvae in the hot moistness of his subconscious mind.

"The habitat has been up and running for six days now," Orr told them. "We've been using an ROV, as I said, for reconnaissance. And yesterday, we launched AUV Orca to gather a detailed surveillance of the city. Data has been coming up in reams, but we have yet to see or even detect a single one of those creatures." He breathed in deeply and exhaled. "They may be there. I don't know. I'm not gonna kid you, we've picked up some strange life-forms down there on sonar, but nobody has seen them in the flesh. Now AUV Orca has done more than just photograph and map the city, it used an industrial laser to cut off a piece of it for examination."

The AUVs, Autonomous Underwater Vehicles, were like extremely high-tech ROVs, except that they were independent, self-governing. When they were deployed, they followed pre-set programming, diving deep and for extended periods of time to complete their mission and then surfacing at a specific point and time to be collected. All without the aid of umbilicals to a mother ship or submersible. They were essentially submarine robots.

Orr opened a box and removed a rectangle of what appeared to be some corrugated black rock. He handed it to Javonivic and she bounced it in her hand and then passed it to Hubbs.

"It's light," he said. "Real light."

"Yes, it is. We've made an analysis of it and fed our findings to the ONR computers."

"What's it made of?" Javonivic wanted to know.

"Mostly granite that was probably quarried from the mountains before they were actually mountains. But it also has a high concentration of a titanium-like alloy and several other unknown metals of low atomic weight in a sort of epoxy-resin. So, basically what this stuff is is a rock/metal/plastic composite. The Labcoat Johnnies at the ONR are baffled. They tell us that the technology to bond something like this does not and potentially cannot exist. Their best guess is that the rocks and metals and plastics were exposed to an incredible heat that turned them molten and bonded them at the molecular level, then the material was molded and machined. At least, that's their guess."

Murphy examined it quickly and then dropped it into Bell's outstretched hand. It was easy to see by the look on his face that he did not like touching it any more than the others had, as if there were memories locked up in it that might become active when in contact with human flesh. He didn't care for the feel of the stuff. It was too smooth and yet too rough. It confused the tactile senses.

But it was only a building material and he tried to remember that. Exotic, yes, but hardly anything to be concerned about.

It was about the size of a small brick and very light. Incredibly so, as if it might float out of his palm if he let go of it. It was black with a greenish shine to it almost like quartz. There was an odd pseudo-machined look to it, its surface raised with tiny bumps and interlocking ridges like it had been cut on a lathe.

He handed it back to Orr who promptly dumped it back in its box and brushed his hands against his khaki pants.

"One last thing," he said. "The AUV did not enter the city; it was not programmed to do so. But it did map out nearly hundreds of possible access points. In a moment, I'll show you what appear to be the best candidates to bring you to the anomaly site. Essentially, that's it, people. Tomorrow morning, you'll go down to the habitat and make preparations to enter the city. I can't tell you what you'll find, but I'm guessing you'll see things no living man ever has, be that good or bad."

But Bell already had a pretty good feeling on that.

There would be wonders in that city, but more so, there would be horror beyond imagination.

4
LAKE VORDOG

The dive team had been 900 feet below the surface of Lake Vordog for three days now. And for Orr sitting above in the Life Support Buoy, the LSB, it had been three long days of wondering and worrying, hoping and fretting.

A lot was riding on this.

He had helmed some pretty hairy operations in his time, but it all paled in comparison to this one. This was a Navy project, yes, but the NSF was the motivating force behind it. They had brought in ONI and ONR—Office of Naval Intelligence and Office of Naval Research, respectively—into this and through them, the massive resources of both the DSU and DSSP were placed at their command under the guise of the Special Projects Office. And that's how Orr had been brought into it.

On paper, the job sounded reasonable enough: drill through the ice to the glacial dome above Vordog, then drop engineering buoys and platform floats onto the lake surface from which the portions of the diver's habitat would be ferried to the bottom via cable descenders, ROVs, and submersibles. Once the dive team was in place, target the submerged city and locate the source of the magnetic anomaly.

And then? Orr didn't know what then. He had sealed orders to be opened once the anomaly was found, but he could pretty much guess.

Just remember the sort of people that are calling the shots on this boondoggle, he reminded himself with a certain amount of anxiety. *What they're capable of and just how expendable you and the team are.*

No, he didn't want to cloud his mind with that.

On paper, the Lake Vordog op sounded like peaches and cream. It didn't get ugly until the entire op was diagrammed out and real-time engineering was factored in. Then…Jesus, it was the biggest thing the DSU had ever undertaken. Those four divers below were what concerned him. He'd gotten them down there and now he wanted to get them back up once the op was successfully completed.

And until then, he couldn't think of anything else.

Standing there in the comm room of the LSB which floated on the surface of Lake Vordog, he puffed on his pipe watching Anderson, his tech, monitor the activities of the dive platform on the bottom. Anderson was the quiet sort. Techies were like that, but Orr knew damn well it was more than just the man's lack of social skills or his mind filled with data that kept him quiet. It was where they were and what was going on below.

Orr walked over to the windows that showed him the surface of Vordog. Even with the exterior lights bathing it, it looked positively black, flat as a sheet of glass. To him, it mattered not that the lake had been tucked beneath the ice for forty-million years. That was for the thinkers. He was a practical man. He saw himself as a working Joe with a job to do. A nuts-and-bolts man. He would let himself see nothing else.

God, the money that had been dumped into this. It staggered the mind.

The entire operation was classified like just about everything the DSU handled, except more so. He wondered what the taxpayers would think if they knew what their government was doing with all those tax dollars.

"Probably wouldn't believe it anyway," he said under his breath.

"Sir?" Anderson said.

"Nothing. Nothing at all."

It had been the engineering job of the century.

First off, the summer before, Kharkov Station had to be refitted. It had been abandoned to the elements for five years and the reason for that depended on what you wanted to believe. And even Orr didn't know the whole truth on that one. Once the station was put back in working order, the drill tower had to be rebuilt. And not the way it was, but something much grander. The original EHWD, Enhanced Hot-Water Drill, had cut a channel through nearly a mile of ice so the ATP cryobot could be released to explore the lake. But that had only required a borehole of about three or four feet in diameter. The borehole the DSU needed had to be some thirty feet in diameter. Big enough to lower the equipment needed to set up the platform and, of course, the platform itself. Once the massive drill tower was built and the new EHWD was put in place, it took weeks to cut a channel like that through the ice.

And when that was done, the real work began.

A winch system was called into action and the equipment was lowered along with engineering buoys and floats, ROVs, submersibles, even living quarters for the DSSD engineering team. Once all that was sorted out and operational, the Neptune Habitat itself was brought down in sections and assembled on a level plateau about three-quarters of a mile from the ancient city. AUV Orca had already selected the site, mapped it out, and dropped sonar markers in place.

The rest was up to the DSSD, Diving System Support Detachment, engineers.

The baseplate for the habitat weighed something like one hundred tons and was lowered to the bottom in twelve sections using tungsten cable guides and balloons that slowly deflated during descent. Once the sections were on the plateau, manned submersibles winched them into place. Divers then bolted them together and welded them into a whole. The baseplate provided anchoring for the habitat as well as a stable and level support base for it. Next, four legs containing 25 tons of lead ballast were fastened to the plate, then leveled using hydraulic-driven screw jacks. Then the habitat vessel itself was attached to the legs. Once it was fitted together, again, piecemeal, it was sealed and pressurized. The entire habitat was completely automated with back-up life support to the point of redundancy. Above, on the surface, the LSB was connected to the Neptune Habitat via steel cables and a three-inch diameter unitized umbilical. The cable contained hoses which supplied air from compressors, oxygen from storage flasks, power lines from generators, as well as coaxial and fiber-optic lines for data and communications.

Everything below could be monitored.

Orr himself had supervised the entire process and he didn't actually believe they'd be able to do it until the moment that the habitat was on-line and operable. Then again, the DSSD had put Neptune Habitats in much deeper water and under worse conditions. They were designed to be easily-deployable. It had taken over two months.

The LSB itself was cavernous. It had something like 70 square meters of inside workspace which did not take into account the outer decks and winches that were used for launching the ROVs and submersibles. It had a communications tower, generators, compressors, VHF radios and a microwave broadcasting system. Half the technology on board was classified. Even when the LSB and Neptune Habitat were warehoused, ready for deployment, it would have been easier to roam the corridors of the Pentagon than it would have been to get within a hundred feet of them. That was the level of secrecy surrounding the DSU's toys.

All that technology, all those resources…and it still did nothing to ease Orr's mind. The margin for human error was always high on a project like this. And especially when you factored in the unknown quantity of who or *what* built that city down there.

Orr sat in his chair and thought about it all. The DSU and DSSP. The DSSD and ONR. ONI and NSF and SPO. AUVs and ROVs. And this while he sat in the comm room of the LSB.

"Fucking alphabet soup," he said under his breath.

"Sir?" Anderson asked.

"Nothing."

There were six civilian techs up in the drill tower monitoring the LSB. Three more that ran Kharkov Station itself. So it wasn't like there was no one around…yet, Orr felt horribly alone. He almost wished they were all down here, feeling what he was feeling. But they were civilians and the Navy didn't want them involved in what were considered the more classified aspects of the op. So they were kept in the dark like Orr's nuts. He only saw a bit more light than they did and he almost wished he was in the dark completely. If what the ONI and NSF had told him at the briefing was in fact true, then ignorance would have been bliss. Because he was starting to believe that there were some things you just didn't want to know about.

"Anderson? Anything from topside?"

The tech shrugged. "Same old, same old, sir. They're monitoring us while we monitor the Neptune."

Orr swallowed. "No…ah…no problems up there?"

"Sir?"

"I mean, there's been no…trouble?"

"I'm not sure what you mean, sir."

"Anything going on up there? Getting any scuttlebutt?"

"No, sir. Nothing."

"Good."

He sat there, feeling like his guts had been tied into sheepshanks and square knots, twisting in on themselves.

He could not shake the feeling that they were not alone here and had not been alone from the moment they arrived at Kharkov. That they were being carefully watched and studied. Sometimes it got so bad, his skin actually crawled. More than once he'd felt those unseen eyes at the nape of his neck so strongly that he'd turned quickly, expecting someone to be there. But there never was, of course. He'd felt that presence up in the station and drill tower, too. But it was stronger down here. Much stronger. And he could just imagine what it might be like down below in that black, weedy lake.

Nerves, it was just goddamn nerves.

You can tell yourself that all you want, but you'll never believe it, he thought. *You can thrust your chest out and say you've seen it all. But you haven't and you know it. What's going on here nobody has seen. And nobody has because they weren't meant to. But it's coming, that ugly moment of cold revelation. And when it arrives and those doors of perception are really thrown open, look out, look out, then Pandora's scabby box will be wide open.*

He re-lit his pipe.

He wondered what it felt like down there. It had to be plenty bad. He knew they were all having those dreams and that dark, cryptic sense of déjà vu. The crew up top were experiencing that stuff, too. Everyone was. Anderson wasn't sleeping much. He claimed his bed was uncomfortable. But that was utter bullshit and Orr knew it. The accommodations on the LSB were first-rate—kid should've tried the beds in Sealab III. *Hell.*

No, it wasn't his bed.

No more than it was Orr's bed that made him wander the decks of the LSB at odd hours. It was the dreams, the headaches, that sense of being watched. The first night, Anderson had cried out in his sleep, but claimed he could not remember what he dreamed about. Again, bullshit. Orr liked to tell himself he couldn't remember those dreams either, but he remembered most of them. God help him, but he did. He didn't talk about them either because maybe talking about them was validating them, admitting they were real and that they scared the shit right out of him.

Last night, Anderson had knocked on Orr's cabin door, wanting to know what the admiral wanted. But Orr didn't want anything. Anderson claimed he'd heard his name called.

Thing was, he probably had.

Orr was certain he'd heard his own name called more than once in a shrill, reedy sort of voice that was almost like a buzzing sound. And maybe Anderson didn't know who was calling him, thought maybe he was hallucinating, but Orr knew better. What was watching them and what was calling them was hiding out there in the darkness. On two separate occasions now, he'd thought he'd seen forms moving about out on the LSB's boat deck. Weird, amorphous sort of shapes that he caught out of the corner of his eye which faded into the gloom when he tried to get a good look.

Oh, they were here, all right.

Same things the hydrobot had filmed below five years before. Down in this black, sepulchral tomb beneath the Vordog ice-dome, they were very much alive, only they did not like to be seen. They were out there even now, staying just beyond the deck lights in that swirling, noxious-smelling mist that clung to the surface of the lake. If you looked into the fog long enough, you would begin to see them as Orr had and even if you did not see them, you would most certainly feel their minds out there, worrying at the edges of your thoughts like psychic buzzards.

He stood up, wiped the sweat off his palms, tapped out his pipe.

Yes, it was bad up here on the surface...but below? Dear God, it must have been like waiting in the womb of hell itself...

5

THE HABITAT

The Neptune Habitat was an 80-ton, double-lock pressure vessel split into two sections: Entry Lock and Main Lock. Each had independent life control systems and could be separately pressurized in case of trouble. Comparing it to Sealab or Hydrolab was like comparing a German V2 rocket to a starship. It was a feat of engineering. As long as the compressors and generators kept operating on the LSB above, the team could have stayed down there six months. And even without the umbilical, the Neptune was self-supporting for several weeks.

Entry Lock was the smaller portion of the module.

It contained the wet porch and moon pool, storage for dive equipment, even hot showers and a whirlpool tub. Entry also had bathrooms, computer work stations, lab space, and life support. Main Lock was much larger. Here were the sleeping quarters, galley, labs, rec room, and the huge bubble viewports. Everything that could possibly be needed.

With the hardsuit diving systems, or *Exosuits* as the Navy called them, you could come in and out of the water with no decompression. This was a wonderful advancement from the days of hyperbaric chambers and awful saturation dives where you had to breathe Heliox, a helium-based mixture of gases.

Everything was in place.

Everything was ready.

And now it would begin.

6

DÉJÀ VU

Although nobody had seen the bogies yet, Bell knew, it did not mean they weren't there. That was his gut feeling on the matter and nothing could convince him otherwise. Javonivic, of course, was not convinced that the creatures still existed. She was quick to espouse her theory that the ones that the hydrobot had filmed five years before might have died out. She was grasping at straws, but that was pure Javonivic. Though she was tough and as experienced as any DSU diver, she could not shake her maternal instincts which were hopelessly optimistic. She mothered the team and refused to accept the fact that there was something out there that could swat them like flies.

"And even if they are there," she said as the four of them lounged in the Main Lock of the Neptune module, "what difference does it really make? We haven't seen them. Maybe they're afraid of us. Maybe they just want to keep away."

Hubbs laughed. "Why in the hell would they be afraid of us, lady? Haven't you heard the spin down here at the Pole? Those things created life on this planet, they created *us*. I can't believe we'd scare them anymore than germs on a Petri dish."

"Why not?" Murphy said. "Frankenstein was afraid of what he created. And you got to admit, people, the human race is a lot scarier than a guy made out of dead parts."

Javonivic smiled, ran a hand through her red buzzcut. "Well, there you go again citing rumors and hearsay and urban legends. Conspiracies. I'll grant you that the aliens were here—"

"Bogies," Murphy said. *"Bogies."*

"—and they might still be. They were obviously extremely intelligent. Even in the Devonian Age, they were light-years beyond where we are now…but there's no hard evidence to validate the claim that they created life or engineered us as a race."

Hubbs barked that laugh again. "Wishful thinking, my dear. They did and we all know it."

"Easy now, Hubbs," Murphy said. "Javy is a creationist. She thinks God made Heaven and Earth and created men in his own image."

Javonivic looked angry. "Can you prove that he or *she* didn't?"

Hubbs shook his head. "Nope. I think God did create us. Only we were a little wrong on his appearance. God happens to be an alien monster, is all."

Bell didn't even bother taking part in it.

The argument was really pointless. Javonivic was essentially right: nobody really knew anything. The aliens existed, or had, they built cities, and they probably played around with the evolution on the planet. Beyond that who really knew? Well, maybe the NSF and the ONI did, but they weren't saying.

He tried not to think about it. Like the argument going on, he tuned it out.

The first day in the habitat had merely been a technical exercise.

The four of them went through the Neptune's systems one by one, checking back ups and redundancies. Then they had secured and performed maintenance on their equipment, everything from the hardsuits to the SDVs, Swimmer Delivery Vehicles. It had been pretty routine stuff, but routine maintenance was the mantra of DSU: if your equipment fails, so does your life expectancy. So, they went over things again and again. As Chief Petty Officer, Bell was in charge of the team. Like Orr himself, he wasn't much on military protocol, but when it came to upkeep and preventative maintenance, he could be a real bastard.

It wasn't until yesterday that they'd actually climbed into their suits and rode the SDVs out to the city itself for reconnaissance. Bell and Murphy had gone in the morning followed by Javonivic and Hubbs in the afternoon. Bell and Murphy had gone again in the evening. And now Hubbs and Javonivic had just returned from yet another survey. Before they tracked the magnetic anomaly, the Navy wanted a general survey of the city itself. AUV Orca had already done much of that, but the divers were to be a little more specific. The whole idea was ridiculous, of course, because the city seemed to go on and on. Much of it had crumbled away into ruins, but the majority, though covered in marine growths, was undamaged.

Bell hated it.

They all hated that damn city even if they were not saying so.

The idea of going back to that graveyard made his stomach clench like a fist. When he'd first seen the photographs of it made five years before, it had literally ripped something open inside him, made him feel like all his stuffing was hanging out. But being in close physical proximity to it was much worse. He had had the headaches, the nausea, the weird dreams and sweaty nightmares just like the rest. The city was somehow catastrophic to the human spirit.

When Murphy and he had first gotten into the belt of ruins outside the city, he'd been scared. And his suit, which monitored his physiology constantly, showed it: racing pulse, accelerated breathing, profuse sweating.

And that was just the outer ruins.

When he got into visual range of the outskirts, he'd had something close to a full-blown panic attack. God, it was like the world's oldest collection of tombs and vaults and megalithic crypts. Rising up above them, the city was fashioned from cubes and blocks, spheres and half-moons and weird geometrical shapes fused into a whole. It was honeycombed with hundreds of passages like rat holes. For a few moments there, he literally couldn't breathe and his heart skipped in his chest. His flesh felt rubbery and chill, his eyes unable to stop staring. He'd experienced the most awful sense of déjà vu he'd ever known. It had filled him and overloaded him.

Javonivic had been on his headset, of course, asking him what the hell was going on. Her monitors back at the habitat were ringing off for both suits. Were they in trouble? It took some time, but Bell assured her they were okay. And this in a voice that sounded like it had been borrowed from a four-year-old girl who'd just shit her pants out of raw terror.

That was his first reaction to it.

What followed was no better. It was as if he was dreaming, lost in some morphic cloud, his mind reeling with images of the city and the bogies. He had glimpses of the city when it was young and filled with creeping life. And that sense of remembrance, again, was beyond mere déjà vu, but a memory of absolute repulsion and horror that was so strong it was positively organic. He *knew* that city...or something inside him did... and it scared him to death.

It was the same for Javonivic and Hubbs, he knew. He heard it in their voices over the comm and saw it in their eyes when they got back: like him, they were haunted by terrible images and twisted half-memories that short-circuited their brains. It was nearly impossible to shut off that high-pitched, demented scream that shrieked from the very core of your being, warning you away from that rising cemetery and what lay within.

And sitting here now, seeing it in his mind black and deranged and invidiously alien, Bell felt cold sweat bead his brow.

It's not right, a voice said in his head. *Nothing about that fucking place is right. I don't care how smart those monsters were, they were evil. Maybe the very seed that inspired what we think of as evil.*

Nothing ever hit him like that before. Nothing had ever kicked him so hard physically, mentally, and even spiritually.

That city is a nightmare, it's a fucking pestilence. And the memory of it is still in you, still in everyone, the ghost that haunts the bones of the race.

Whatever interactions humans—or what might *become* humans—had with those creatures and that city it must have been horrible beyond belief to still linger on so strongly.

Because Bell knew a little something about fear reactions.

As a sailor involved in a profession that was extremely dangerous and outright suicidal at times, he had been gone over by the best psychologists in the business. The DSU allowed no one in their ranks that were remotely nervous or indecisive. He knew that there were two kinds of fear: learned and inherited. You learned to fear nuclear radiation, shotguns pointed in your face, and terrorists because you were taught they were dangerous. But no one had to teach you to fear a growling dog or a hissing snake or the depths of a dark cave…it was inherited. It was part of your preprogrammed survival kit developed by countless generations of experience from your ancestors. Growling dogs could bite you; snakes could be poisonous; dark caves hid predators. And like that, no one had to tell him that the city and what lived in it was dangerous: he *knew* it. The memory was ingrained in him.

He wanted to destroy it.

And although the orders to do so were still sealed, he knew that's what this mission was about. They all did. For stored safely in lockboxes were enough hybrid RDX Comtac explosives to flatten Midtown Manhattan. And, honestly, Bell had all he could do not to use them.

As if reading his mind, Hubbs said, "Let's not dick around, people. When we find that anomaly and document it, we're going to destroy it. Simple as that. I don't know what this is all about, but I can guess. And my guess is that the Pentagon wants to borrow some of the…*bogies'* technology to be used as weapons."

"You can't know that," Javonivic said.

"No, but it's my guess."

Neither she nor Hubbs had said much about what they saw at the city. They didn't really have to, of course, because the hardsuits had onboard video that was sent back to the Neptune. Everything the divers saw appeared on the monitors. But there was something else. Everyone who came back from that place looked a little pale, a little shaken, but Javonivic more so. She kept looking at Bell like she wanted to get him alone, say things she couldn't in front of Hubbs.

"Your theory is full of holes, Hubbs," she said. "Realistically, what makes you think they have any technology we could use? Their origin and evolution are obviously in great contrast to our own. They may have nothing we can use or if they do, there might be no way we can possibly harness it. I heard that stuff that came out of Kharkov. Those two survivors said the bogies' technology was organically-based with a varying degree of supportive hardware. What the hell are we going to do with organic technology? Nothing, that's what."

Hubbs smirked. "Oh, come now, Javy. You underestimate human

inventiveness. If these creatures have something we can use as a weapon, we'll figure out a way to exploit it. We're very inventive when it comes to killing our own kind."

"No, they're too advanced, too different. We always expect aliens to be like us. That there'd be some exchange of ideas, but that's silly. The Elder Things…*bogies*…are too different. They do not strike me as having been overly mechanized or industrial. That city…as much of a freak show as it is…almost looks like a marine growth itself. I don't think these creatures are like us. They do not wantonly destroy or damage their environment, but shape it to fit their own needs. They work with it, learn from it. We can't even grasp their sense of technology."

"Oh, boy. You hear that, Chief?" Hubbs said. "Javy wants to shake hands with 'em, take me to your leader."

She sighed. "I'm just saying we're talking apples and oranges. They have no need of our technology and we couldn't even begin to translate theirs. No, boys, I haven't seen them and maybe they're dead or afraid of us, but just because they might offend us physically, it doesn't mean they're monsters. We're like children to them. And any wise parent does not give children weapons to kill other children with. Maybe we can learn from them, but not about warfare."

Hubbs gave up. "Time to check in with Orr."

That left the three of them there. They sat in silence a moment, uncomfortable silence. Finally, Bell said, "Okay, Javy. Let's have it."

She looked around, then lowered her voice, "Hubbs is acting weird, Chief. I don't like it. Last night, I found him staring out the viewport into the lake. I asked him what he was doing and he just smiled at me. And the way he smiled gave me the creeps. And today out at the city, he stuck real close to me. We're supposed to stay in VR, you know, Visual Range and all that…but he was acting like a scared schoolboy. I think he saw something, only he won't say what."

"Maybe it's what he saw in the viewport yesterday," Murphy said.

But that was still open to debate—they didn't know if he *had* seen anything. Hubbs had let out a cry and everyone came running. He was scared white, backing away from the port like something out there was going to get him. Again, he wouldn't say what it was.

"He saw something," Murphy said. "I mean, c'mon, you know the guy. He's like iron. Shit, before yesterday, I didn't even know he *could* be afraid."

Javonivic said, "This place is getting to all of us. I'm getting the spooks myself. But it's worse with him. I just can't get past the idea that he saw something in the city."

Murphy studied his hands. "Maybe he did. And worse, maybe it saw him, too."

7
ENCOUNTER

Orr said nothing to Anderson.

He let him occupy himself with the battery of technology at the console. He walked out of the comm room quietly, calmly, drawing no attention to himself. They usually spent five hours on and five hours off at the console. Of course, both of them were pretty much on all the time because they couldn't sleep worth a damn and what sleep they did get was not exactly restful.

Orr pulled on his parka and gloves, walked outside and stood there, staring at the decks and the lights holding back the gloom and mist. There was no sound. Nothing but an occasional drip of water or a distant cracking of the ice. Like some great soundless, black vacuum where everything was shifted into neutral. Without even starlight or weather, only that oppressive mist gathering to all sides, even time didn't seem to exist. The world, as it were, was a stygian void.

Orr thought: *Well, you gonna stand here like a wallflower waiting for a dance or are you gonna do this thing?*

Sighing, he stepped out on deck, scanning his eyes back and forth. His footsteps were loud on the metal deck plates. Tensing, he moved out near the ROV which sat yellow and bulbous on its platform, the winch cables securing it wet and glistening from the moist air. He looked up and could only see darkness, but he knew that somewhere up there was the borehole leading up to the drill tower a mile above.

Although the deck lighting which burned constantly—didn't dare turn it off, God no–lit up things pretty good, it was still shadowy out there with the mist snaking along the plating and drifting before the mounted halogens. Orr pulled out his flashlight and played the beam over the equipment and derricks crowded everywhere. Shadows danced around him.

He swallowed, found his voice. "If you're out here, show yourself."

His voice echoed off and was consumed by the fog, buried alive in its weight. The fog was thick, white, and fuming. It did not seem to move really. It shivered, trembled, but that was about it. It almost seemed static. A great, dense pall that was somehow ghostly and oozing like ectoplasm, not really solid, but not really gaseous either. It was created by the cold air of the glaciers striking the warm surface of the lake. If you stood on the decks and watched, you could see it rising from the black water like steam off a pot. It was blank and eerie.

He'd seen something out here.

He knew he had.

And something substantial this time, not just some fog-phantom like you saw if you stared into mist for any length of time, your mind creating shapes where none existed. No, this had been real. Again, like so many times before, he had caught it out of the corner of his eye. But this time, there was no denying its reality.

It had been there.

A black, nebulous shape fading into shadow.

The bank of compressors on the far end of the LSB started up and he nearly jumped out of his skin. They cycled on and off at regular intervals, sending oxygen down to the Neptune.

He waited for about five minutes and they turned back off.

He moved around the ROV, his light reflecting off the mist, shining off the water that was flat as the surface of a mirror. He saw a few looming shapes out there and his heart began to pound...but they were just the DSSD engineering floats moored to the LSB.

"I feel like a kid in a haunted house waiting for a ghost," he whispered.

And that was pretty much it: he knew the spooks were here, he could feel them, sense their closeness...just not see them. He panned his light over the mist. Nothing. The beam picked out the shape of the AUV Orca tethered to the LSB. A lingering, acrid smell came off the lake. He wrinkled his nose.

Water dripped somewhere.

His heart began to race. He wasn't sure what it was at first, nerves maybe, but it did not subside: it increased. In his gloves, his hands felt sweaty. Teardrops of moisture ran down his face. A dank chill moved up his spine.

He heard a sound that made him turn around fast: a low droning sound like a swarm of midges.

He did not move. For maybe twenty seconds, he did not even breathe. He just stood there, the dank mist rising around him, the flashlight gripped tightly in one gloved hand. His whole body was minutely trembling. The sound of that droning, like a hovering cloud of mating insects, made his flesh creep.

It came again, louder this time.

From out in the mist.

From maybe a dozen places like separate swarms of insects were calling out to one another. And then it came yet again, but this time it was behind him: clear, distinct, unnerving. He knew he had to turn around and face the thing. He'd wanted to see it…at least, some part of him did…and now here was his chance. He could feel it back there, hear the hollow sound of its respiration, the leathery scraping of its limbs. And smell it, yes, dear God, he could smell it—a pungent, acrid odor like methyl alcohol and chemical preservatives that made his nose burn.

His chest was so tight, his lungs contracted with fear, that breathing was like trying to suck air through a swamp reed. He swallowed, said in a choked voice, "Anderson…is that you?"

That low droning rose up again. It was like the soundtrack to a jungle swamp, but infinitely sinister.

In his head, Orr heard, *turn around and face me*…not a voice, but a searing thought, but one he did not think that his own mind had generated. He swung around, wishing he'd brought a gun, and looked his visitor dead-on.

The first glimpse made him feel weak and loose inside.

Dear God…

It droned at him, directly at him, and that sound stirred a panic like he'd never known before. Not even when he'd been a salvage diver and had gotten trapped beneath the hull of a freighter in six-hundred feet of water off Long Island Sound. There had been panic then, too, that he overcame with sheer guts and training, but this was beyond that. If that had been like burning cordite flaring inside him, this was like an atomic bomb going off. The panic rose right up from the cellar of his being and sucked the wind right out of him.

The creature.

It was about twelve feet from him, close enough that its rank smell was shoved down his throat and he could see the droplets of water beading on its blue-gray, oily hide. It hovered over the deck like a ghost from an evil fairy tale, water dripping from it.

But it was no ghost.

It was very large and very three-dimensional. Its body was barrel-shaped, set with elongated vertical ridges that gave its torso a geometrical look like something machined, artificial. Its walking legs, or tentacles beneath, whatever they were, dangled like the pale roots of a dead orchid. Great membranous wings projected from either side of the body, spread wide like Chinese fans. Orr could see the bony architecture of spines that held them in place. At the top of its body was a head, a starfish-like head, the fleshy projections of which reminded him of the arms of a candelabra, a brilliant red eye at the apex of each. Those eyes—all five of them—were perfectly round and wet, a tiny pinprick pupil set in each.

In the flesh, the bogie was perfectly alien and perfectly hideous.

Orr tried to breathe, to keep standing, to do a lot of things.

Although it made no indication that it would hurt him, he knew it could crush him like a bug. His mind began to clear, all those neurotic racial memories quieting, and he stood his ground. The thing made a droning sound like maybe it was speaking to him. There were squirming parasites running down the lower section of its torso, making it look as if it was infested by worms. It had two limbs midline of its body...weird, branching things like sticks, though rubbery and boneless. They tapered into clusters of tendrils like fingers. It rubbed the limbs together and there was a crackling sound like dry cellophane.

Although he did not think it possible, he found his voice and said, "What…what in the Christ do you want?"

And that was the question, wasn't it?

Because it made no threatening gestures. It just hovered there like some great insect, wings spread out, dripping and staring and making an occasional crackling sound with its limbs. Out in the mist, more droning noises came from at least a dozen different locations. The thing droned back, maybe calling to the others. Orr could feel the heat of its mind brush his own, but only in a curious sort of way. It was not afraid of him. It seemed to enjoy looking at him, maybe trying to understand why he was not terrified of it. It just kept staring and staring like he was a germ under a microscope.

And you ain't much more to that monster.

He made no moves at it.

The ball was in the creature's court.

If it wanted him, it would take him. Simple as that. He knew it was reading his mind and he was only glad he could not read its own. As he looked upon it, he felt pure animal aggression stir inside him. He hated it. There was nothing more, just hatred. He wanted to kill it. He wanted to have a gun in his hand so he could drill holes through it. Because he knew one thing: the history of this creature and the history of his own race were intertwined and it had never, ever been a dance of joy. It had been dark and ugly and horrible. This thing was the absolute nemesis of his race and he longed to murder it as all men secretly, subconsciously, did.

It droned again.

Orr, not really thinking, brought up the flashlight and put the beam in its eyes. It moved backward a few feet with a brief swish of its wings. He did not know how it hovered like that, but it seemed to take no physical exertion that he could see.

The hatred he felt overwhelmed him. "Well, here I am. What the fuck do you want?"

It droned and flared its wings.

And Orr acted instinctively.

Maybe it was going to attack and maybe it wasn't. Regardless, his animal instinct spiked and he threw the flashlight at it with everything he had. It passed right through it as if it was made of smoke. Instantly, the creature pulled away, its wings flapping in a blur with a shrill buzzing sound. Its eyes seemed to burn even brighter…and then it simply slipped off into the fog and dissipated. It became ghostly, almost transparent, and he could see the fog through it. Then it broke apart into something like a cloud of fireflies that winked out one by one.

A ghost. A fucking ghost.

Out in the mist, there was a solid wall of droning and then nothing.

Orr went right down on his ass, his heart hitching painfully, his bladder so full he thought he'd piss right down his leg. His heart found its rhythm again and he sat there, breathing, trying to convince himself it was all some fucked-up hallucination brought on by the gases in the mist, but he knew better. He could still smell the thing.

He wasn't sure how long he sat there, his breath frosting out in clouds, but he heard the hatch open and Anderson came running out.

"Sir! Sir? Sir…are you all right?"

And Orr had a crazy impulse to laugh. "Sure, all things considered, I'm doing quite well."

PARANOID

When he was finally alone in his cabin, away from prying eyes and listening ears (or so he hoped), Hubbs finally relaxed. He sat down on his bunk and sighed, knowing he had to pull himself together, knowing he was here to do a job, and knowing that he was a professional with hundreds of hours of deep-saturation dives under his belt. And with all that, it should have been doable if not exactly easy.

Yet, as soon as his ass hit the cushion of the bunk, it was as if all the muscles inside him had gone limp and loose. He had all he could do to stay upright. His mouth was dry. His hands shaking. His limbs boneless.

And as this occurred, a small voice that seemed to come from somewhere south of his rational brain, said, *They're talking about you right now and you know it. They were just waiting for you to leave. It's Javy. Fucking Javy. She's leading the charge. She's been acting weird around you ever since you got back from the city. She suspects you of…of something.*

His forearm itched madly and he scratched it manically, fiercely through the sleeve of his jumpsuit. As he did so, he thought about Javonivic. She'd always had his back. Maybe they'd never been exactly close (he didn't even know where she'd been born or anything about her beyond the most basic generalities), but they worked together well in the DSU. One op after another, they'd gotten the job done. They were pros.

But now…God, he just didn't know. This whole Lake Vordog thing was one for the books, all right. It was hard to gauge it objectively because they'd never been involved in anything like this. Orr had put it best when he told them, *"The…bigness of this one is more than a little overwhelming."* And that was it exactly: the *bigness* of it. Things were happening down here. Things in the shadows or behind your back or just behind the scenes.

Hubbs knew that much.

Everyone was acting a bit off. He figured they were all scared like he was, but being DSU, they'd never admit it in a million years.

Oh, there' so many things no one will admit to.

Himself included. That was the problem with an outfit like the DSU—things were very rigid, protocol set in stone. If you deviated from that, you were out. The Navy brass didn't fuck around. They expected you not only to be in perfect physical fitness, but mentally balanced and solid as a rock. And if Hubbs was to admit to the things he'd seen, well, it would all go down in his file (Bell would see to that) and his career would end right there.

Trust, he thought, *there's no trust now.*

They all wanted to know what he'd seen the other day through the viewport that made him cry out. They'd all come running, pegging him with questions that he did not dare answer. What would they have said if he had told them about it? About any of it? That he'd seen something staring in at him or that last night he'd seen a figure out there. The figure of a man floating in the lake. No suit on, just a white, bloated corpse that looked as if it had been in the water a week. As he watched, it slowly began to flake away into a maelstrom of particles and fragments. All of which was bad enough, but it had worn his face.

They'd say he was nuts, that's what.

And maybe, just maybe, they'd be right.

He sat there, thinking, trying to come to terms with himself. Who he was and, just maybe, *what* he was. Everything was scattered. He was like a puzzle now that was missing pieces. Had they always been missing? Had he ever truly been whole? Had he always been broken and fractured like this? He realized at that moment that he needed a drink like he'd never needed one before. Something wet in his mouth, cooling his throat, warming his belly and soothing his head. The terrible craving made him feel like he was dry and shriveled inside, cracked open like arid soil. That was crazy, of course, because he wasn't much of a drinker. A beer now and again. Maybe a few icy glasses of Sangria when he was out to dinner with friends. That was it...but, oh Christ, how he needed a drink.

He couldn't stop thinking about what he'd seen outside the viewport. He wasn't even sure what had drawn him to look out of it in the first place. Only that, later, as he thought it over, he was certain that it had not been a conscious decision on his part. It was almost as if he had been *made* to look out there. The first thing he had seen had not been that awful figure, but his reflected image in the glass. It had startled him. The face he knew so well—the cocky leer of his eyes (which his mother had lovingly called *roguish*), his perpetually smirking mouth, the sunburned cheeks he'd sported since his teenage surfing years in Oceanside—was gone, replaced by a catatonic, grim visage that appeared decades older than it actually was.

That's when he noticed the floating figure out there, staring at him with empty eye sockets from a puffy, fish-nibbled face. It slowly broke apart, dissolving like salt dumped in water until it was just a swirling, milky cloud of matter that, too, dissipated.

That's when he'd cried out and the others came running to find him standing there, his face greased with sweat, his body trembling, eyes opaque with fear.

You better hide it from them or they won't trust you anymore, he'd thought.

But could he hide it from Javy?

In the city, something impossible and downright insane had happened. He'd blanked. Inside his suit, he'd felt something, a change in pressure, a sense that the self-contained atmosphere had become poisoned. He tried to tell Javy about it, but she wasn't there. One moment, she'd been five feet away and then she was just gone. He found himself trapped in an encompassing bank of seaweed or hydroids, perhaps even both. They were formed of countless yellow-green spirals that wound around him, sharp pink tendrils erupting from them. They brushed against his suit, dragging over the view plate bubble like hundreds of tapering pink fingers. He had panicked, trying to fight his way free, but they held him, snaring him up like the net of a fisherman. The terrible thing was, that he could feel them *inside* his suit, stinging his arm like the tentacles of a jellyfish.

It was impossible.

There was no way they could have gotten in his hardsuit, yet he could feel them, the burning sensation in his forearm. The tendrils felt rubbery, sticky, their tips sharp as needles.

Then they were gone and Javy was asking him if he was okay. What could he say? Threaded with terror, he told her he was just fine.

But he couldn't tell the others about that. It was simply too far out. Yet, for all that and as absurd as the idea was, he couldn't stop itching at his forearm incessantly.

9
NIGHTMARE

That night, Hubbs slept uneasily, tossing and turning, limbs trembling and sweat beading his face. His body jerked stiff as a post, then folded up like a jackknife. He was unaware of any of it, of course, or that there was a presence in the room, watching him, water dripping from it steadily.

He dreamed he was approaching the city and Javonivic was at his side. They moved together, slowly jetting forward over the rubble and ruin of the outskirts that were not shattered walls and arches and broken domes, but leaning gravestones like those in some medieval European cemetery. They were encrusted with barnacles and draped with green kelp that undulated in a secret current, waving side to side. They pushed on, the beams of their lights like yellow swords cutting through the murk and suspended sediment. Then the city was right before them and it looked just like the witch's castle in a book of fairy tales from his early childhood—tall, narrow, grotesque and twisted, a collection of sharp-peaked roofs and skeletal spires.

In the dream, he heard a voice that sounded much like his own tell him that the city was the source of all the terrors he had known as an infant in his crib when the world around him was cyclopean and menacing.

He wanted to turn back. In fact, it was paramount that he turn back, but Javy would not have it. She pulled him through the doorway of the city which, again, was like the doorway of the witch's castle: a gigantic headstone-shaped wooden door with rusting iron hasps that creaked when they opened it.

Inside, they moved through a forest of tall, snaking reeds and crawling seaweed. They were not alone. Unseen forms glided through the weeds, following them, darting around them.

"She's coming," Javy said, her voice weak with fear. "She's coming for us now."

"Who?" Hubbs wanted to know. "Who is coming?"

"My mother. She killed me so my father could eat me," she said and he recognized this as something from a fairy tale, too. "My bones were gathered in a silken scarf and laid beneath the juniper tree."

Then he saw a shape coming through the weeds, a female shape that he knew must be her mother. It was draped in marine growths, sea slugs filling its open mouth. It held out hands that were the slimy tentacles of a mollusk reaching for him.

When the time is right, she said through the mouth of slugs, *you'll see me for what I am.*

When he woke, he was moaning, scratching at his forearm. The itching was terrible, like a collection of dozens of mosquito bites. He pulled his arm frantically from the sleeve of his jumpsuit and saw that where the seaweed had stung him there was a patch of pink scales like those of a carp.

And from the shadows, he heard a voice say, *"Tweet, tweet, what a beautiful bird am I..."*

Hubbs threw himself off the bed, his skin crawling, seeming to creep on the bones beneath. As beads of sweat rolled down his face and systemic shock made him nearly pass out, he saw that there was no one there but him.

He was losing his mind.

10
MOTHER REGINA

In the wet porch of the Neptune, Javonivic watched Bell and Murphy being hoisted over the open moon pool by the hydraulic winch, Hubbs at the controls. The moon pool was circular, about twenty feet in diameter, and was the entry/exit port for the divers going into the lake and coming out of it. Only the pressurized atmosphere kept the water from filling the habitat.

He centered them over the pool.

In their huge, articulated Exosuits that resembled very elaborate pale blue suits of armor, they looked like robots ready to explore an alien world. And, really, that's what they were doing.

On her headset, she said, "You boys ready to get wet?"

"Ready," Bell said over the radio.

"Sure," Murphy said, "she only asks me that when I got my suit on."

"Lower," she told Hubbs.

The winch gradually dropped the divers into the pool. Their helmets disappeared and there were a few bubbles, then nothing. The winch claw released them below and they swam off, powered by the hardsuit jets, making for the SDV tethered to one of the Neptune's legs.

"Well," Hubbs said when the winch claw was up out of the water, "now the fun begins."

"What do you mean by that?"

He secured the winch with the toggle control, killed the power to it. He laughed. "What do I mean, she asks. We're down at the bottom of a lake beneath a fucking glacier in Antarctica and she wants to know what I mean." He folded his arms. "What do you think I mean? Those boys are going out to an alien city, Javy. And I get the feeling that city ain't as dead as we might like it to be."

"There's no evidence of that."

"I got all the evidence I need."

She sighed. "Please share it."

"C'mon, Javy. Stop being so damn naïve. You feel that place same as I do. It's not dead. It's far from dead. And the things that built it are still there, watching us."

She rolled her eyes. "Unfortunately, your assessment of the situation is somewhat lacking. There's not one scrap of evidence that the bogies are still active or that they mean us any harm."

Hubbs offered her a twisted grin. "I'm not talking about the Old Ones or Elder Things or whatever the hell you want to call them. I'm talking about something else."

"What?"

"I'm not sure," he said, swallowing. "The city itself. It's not dead. Not the way it should be. There's…I don't know…a sort of life to it. I've felt it and so have you."

"That's crazy."

"Is it? C'mon, Javy. Quit with the bullshit. That city is not just a city. It's something more and you know it. It watches us all the time. I think it can get into our minds, into our dreams."

"Now you're guessing." Though she never would have admitted it, what he said unnerved her because she'd thought the same thing herself. And more than once.

He shrugged. "You've felt it, Javy. I know you have."

"I haven't felt anything."

It was Hubbs' turn to roll his eyes. "Don't be such a fucking Pollyanna, okay?"

"I'm not a Pollyanna."

"Sure thing, Pollyanna."

She glared at him. "I don't appreciate being called that."

He smiled thinly. "Javy, Javy, Javy. Now, where have we gone wrong with you? You've been in that fucking tomb with me. You've felt the dread of that place. The danger. It's a nightmare just like the things that built it. Can you deny it? If you can, your mother should have taught you better."

"You leave my fucking mother out of this!" she snapped.

Hubbs gave her a pitying look, wondering, apparently, what nerve he'd touched. He left the wet porch, making for the Main Lock and the control room. And good riddance to him. When he went through the airlock, she showed him one of her less Pollyanna-type attributes: she flipped him off.

Now you did it, she thought. *You let him push your buttons. You lost control. You showed him your soft white underbelly and that prick will remember it, too.*

She buried her face in her hands, shaking. Yes, of course, he was right—she'd felt the menace of the city, felt it digging deep into her. She'd been moody and bitter ever since her first trip there, her emotions just under the skin like tinder waiting to burn. *And scared, oh God in heaven, don't forget about the terror you've felt.* She was not herself. It was like there was another Javonivic inside her, a terrified, deranged anti-Javonivic that screamed in her head. An animal in a cage.

Hubbs knew it, too.

Somehow, he did.

But the city is just a city, regardless of how abstract it is…it can't be alive, it can't toy with our minds and dreams. Do you really believe that?

She just didn't know. Her sense of logic told her the very idea was absurd, yet her emotions, her instinct, told her otherwise.

"Hubbs is an asshole," she whispered. "He's trying to mess with you."

She clenched her teeth, feeling the world—*her* world—spinning out of control. Guys like Hubbs were hateful, cynical savages at their core. They fed, they fucked, they killed, they shit. But there was no poetry in them, no spirituality. They were exactly what the Old Ones had engineered humans to be: soulless brutes that could be easily manipulated. She saw people like him as a lower order, things barely one step from the caves.

Oh God, what was happening? No, she'd never exactly been in love with Hubbs. But she'd never hated him like this either.

She shouldn't have let him provoke her...but that goddamn crack about her mother, harmless though it was, had been like a hot knife sliding into her guts. She did not like to think about her mother because she had been too much like Hubbs.

That's always been your problem, Alice, Regina Javonivic, the Great and Terrible, said. *You think like a boy, you act like a boy. But there's nothing swinging between your legs, in case you haven't noticed. Try being the woman God intended you to be. Find purpose. Find a man and let him take care of you. Have some children and quit pretending you have a penis.*

"No, goddammit," Javonivic said out loud, immediately clasping a hand to her mouth.

No, no, no. This wouldn't do. She wouldn't let that awful bitch torment her and traumatize her as she had when she was a teenager. She had worked hard to be where she was now, a member of the elite DSU. She had succeeded in a profession ruled by men and she would not let that bitch take it all away from her now.

The idea was unacceptable.

You exorcised her years ago, Javonivic thought. *Why are you letting her get to you now that she's been dead ten years?*

That was the question, wasn't it? The very one that she fought with day in and day out. Her mother (she didn't much care to refer to Regina by that term) still had a hold on her. From beyond the grave, that evil witch was still tormenting her. Javonivic made herself calm down. Regina was dead. She was powerless. If anyone was truly tormenting her, it was herself and she knew it.

But the memories of Regina were carved into her soul, electroplated onto her brain. Even on those days when she successfully purged that awful woman from her conscious mind, she was never really gone; she was merely hiding in the cobwebbed sub-cellar of her subconscious, a monster skulking in the shadows under the stairs waiting to reach out and grab her.

Javy's childhood had been shit.

Her father died when she was five (lost at sea in a fishing boat, or so she was told) and that's when Regina's reign of terror began. Maybe the siege itself didn't really begin until she was ten or so, the true devastation and bloodshed being her teenage years, but it had been apparent that something was off about her mother from her earliest memories. That narrow, pallid face, those hot eyes that would burn right through you.

Sitting there, Javy realized she was breathing hard, beads of sweat on her brow.

The torment itself was rarely physical, mostly psychological, but it had been horrendous. Physical scars healed, but the ones slashed into the psyche of a young, impressionable girl never went away. They scabbed over, yes, but sooner or later, she picked at them because she couldn't help herself and then the poisoned blood ran hot and feverish.

When Javy was sixteen, Regina was no more. The details of her death were sketchy at best. Regina hated the sea. It terrified her, made her angry, was a source of endless paranoia to her. Then one day, she'd rowed out into it, never to be seen again. She'd borrowed their next-door neighbor's twelve-foot rowboat. That much was known. The boat washed ashore three days later and Regina's body was never found.

The hows and whys of all that were never explained. They could not be understood. Why would someone with that complete terror of the sea take a rowboat out onto it? Then again, why would someone who was terrified of the ocean live on the shore? What sense did that make? But of course, Regina made no sense. It was probably rooted in what happened to Javy's father, but she learned better than to dare ask. Regina would stand in the kitchen in the dead of night with a single candle burning and stare out into the primeval vastness of the Atlantic. Sometimes, she'd walk out there in the darkness just before sunrise and stand at the very edge of the beach where the low tide had stranded all the dead things, seemingly watching for something no one else could see.

And on those few occasions when Javy dared ask her why, Regina had grabbed her like a sand crab seizing a fish. *"Because I have to. Somebody has to keep watch. Somebody has to be alert because it can happen at any time, Alice. Sooner or later, they always return for their own."* That was it. An esoteric statement with no explanation.

Yes, she had been a woman of great contradictions and deep-set fears you did not want to know about. But what had been her plan when she rowed out there? Had it been suicide? Was that how Regina Javonivic wanted to go out, at the very mercy of the thing she feared most? Nobody knew. Particularly not Javy who'd gone to live with her aunt in St. Michaels.

The entire episode traumatized her, of course. There was no true sense of closure. She used to lie in her bed at night, listening to the ocean, imagining that Regina was out there, waiting. That she was somewhere in the deeps, tangled in seaweed, infested by sea snails and bivalves. Bristle worms living in her eyes and hagfish tunneling into her belly. A puffed, white, rotten thing chewed by squid, forever staring with eyes like hot glass, grinning with a mouth of black mud. And that some dark night when the dankness blew in off the sea, she'd come back and stand over her bed, dripping sea slime and rank saltwater.

"Enough," she said. "Enough."

She stood there, staring down into the moon pool. The lights below illuminated the baseplate of the Neptune. She stared, almost fixated, not knowing what she was waiting for. Or maybe she did and this was what made her finally look away, her throat suddenly dry as chalk.

"Quit with the heebie-jeebies," she told herself. "You're here to do a job. That's all. Just another job. Man up."

It sounded good, at any rate. At least until she remembered the dreams she'd been having, that inescapable sense that she was being watched. Or that terrible shape she sometimes glimpsed hovering about the viewports. Imagination and stress, a little of both, but that did not dispel the awful, crawling feeling in her belly that told her that this place was akin to a graveyard at midnight and the dead were not resting easily.

She simply could not shake it.

The dreams, God, those awful dreams of pure terror. They were like a drill bit piercing her skull. Though she could never exactly remember the specifics, the awfulness of them stayed with her for hours, making her feel small and vulnerable, filled with a deep gnawing anxiety she could not shake. The only thing she could truly recall was a terrible, skin-crawling feeling of scratching in her head as if her brain was an egg getting ready to hatch, some unformed, embryonic horror waiting to be born.

She had never been neurotic by nature, but, God, it was getting worse by the day.

You need to calm down, to center yourself.

Yes, that was it exactly.

She needed to remember who she was and what she was. There was no room for superstition or childlike terrors. She cleansed it from her mind by concentrating on the job itself.

She was honored that Orr had chosen her, handpicked her from the elite ranks of the DSU. This whole op was incredible, to say the least.

The technology was cutting edge, much of it strictly classified.

This was wonderful and new.

But it did little to lift her spirits.

She just stood there, not sure what she was thinking and less sure of what she was feeling. Again, she should have been happy. This whole op was the opportunity of a lifetime for a deep submergence diver. A sub-glacial lake that had been locked away from the outside world for forty million years. And if that wasn't enough, there was a city down here built by an alien race in prehistory. Her team was the first to make a comprehensive survey of that relic and of the lake itself. She should have been wild with excitement and scientific wonder—but she wasn't. Because it was all wrong and she knew it. It was bad enough when she was awake, but the nightmares that came when she closed her eyes…no, this whole thing was just wrong.

You're being superstitious, she calmly told herself. *You're being an unreasoning, confused, emotive savage like Hubbs. That's what you're being.*

But how could she help it?

How could she help any of it?

This place scared her like nothing before in her life. It made her feel small and fearful and panicky. Trapped, held in a cage. Like a bug on a pin slowly being impaled deeper and deeper.

The lake was fascinating, yes. Plenty of life. She had seen very little of it, but it was there. Forms that existed nowhere else on Earth. Still, she was scared. It wasn't the great depths or local wildlife or even the desolation of this place, this sunken primordial world, but that goddamn city. It was like a haunted house dropped to the lake bottom: deserted and surreal and skeletal, leering out at you like a skull in the desert. She knew that if she was alone down there with it, she would have most certainly slit her wrists.

And how was that for unscientific?

Sighing, she stared down into the moon pool, feeling the weight of it all pressing down on her and threatening to squeeze her flat. She thought about Bell and Murphy and where they were going and what they were going to do.

She touched the crucifix at her throat. "Oh, God," she said, "we need you now more than ever."

11
THRESHOLD

The closer they got to it, the murkier the water became.

Of course, the entire lake was pitch-black save for a few phosphorescent colonies of marine life that clung to the rocks down in jagged crevices on the bottom. But the closer they got—and Bell did not need instrumentation to tell him that they were nearing it, he could feel it in his belly—the more sediment was suspended in great clouds like fluffy motes of dust. The SDV's twin props pushed them through fields of it where there was absolutely no visibility. Inside his hardsuit, riding on the SDV, it made him feel claustrophobic. Even the lights of his suit and the powerful halogen lamps of the craft itself were useless. The SDV had onboard obstacle avoidance sonar, so there was never any danger of running into a shelf of rock or a jutting seamount…yet the claustrophobia was markedly real and tenacious.

And maybe it wasn't the sediment so much as the idea that something had kicked it up.

Something they could not see.

Welcome to the world of Lake Vordog.

Even with the lights, it was like being in the world's darkest cave, zipped tight in a body bag. When they cleared the sediment, it wasn't so bad. Clumps of it clung to the aluminum shells of their suits like peat moss, but at least the lights could show them things.

The lake bottom was flat in places, in others, deep cut by submarine canyons that sonar told them dropped for hundreds of feet. There were rises and valleys, outcropping of glossy black volcanic rocks and cave mouths far below where schools of bioluminescent squids played and cavorted. They saw great clusters of pillar-shaped sponges and forests of brown kelp, inching mud worms and white cup-shaped mollusks. What looked to be tangled masses of large, feathery bright-red brittle stars and giant tube worms with puckered, sucking mouths. Trenches filled with colonies of orange- and yellow-tentacled sea whips and anemones. And once, several gigantic albino arthropods that were perfectly ghastly with their segmented legs and antennae and bizarre claws. Like something from a Roger Corman movie.

There was plenty of life.

And plenty of death.

Gullies were filled with the picked shells of mussels and clams, the bloated carcasses of long, finless eel-like fish which were being fed upon by tiny crustaceans and slinking flatworms.

Over the com, Bell said, "You still reading low salinity in the lake?"

"Absolutely, Chief," Murphy told him.

"Makes no sense. Marine forms everywhere down here. Shouldn't be anything like this in fresh water."

"Nature has a way of adapting when the need arises."

Yes, Vordog was very much alive and there were plenty of other things, shapes and elongated forms, that swam about at the edges of their lights, curious but frightened away by the brightness. Some of them were very large, even larger than the men themselves in their huge robotic suits. Bell didn't know what they were, but he'd seen those darting shapes on his previous runs. They could have been just about anything, but he knew one thing they were not: Old Ones. Because if they had been, he would have known it. He would have felt it.

Now and again, Javonivic would come over the radio and ask, "How's the trip, boys?"

"Peachy," Murphy would say.

"Seeing anything?"

And Murphy would say, "You know I only have eyes for you."

"Oh, that's so sweet. If you were here, I'd wrap my legs right around you."

"Damn…can you wait until I get back?"

"Nope. I'll take care of myself by then."

"Bitch."

And she'd laugh. But that laughter was always slightly brittle, forced. Because she knew where they were and what they were facing. It was bad enough in the habitat, but out here…you felt so unprotected. Like something might make a snack of you at any moment.

Bell had never felt that before.

He'd been down in abyssal depths salvaging sunken subs or ships and had seen gigantic, profuse forms moving at the perimeter of the lights. Giant squid maybe, but they had not scared him. Nothing scared him like this place did. It got inside you, filled your belly with a black, creeping gestation that turned everything inside you sour, absolutely owned you at some primal level.

Maybe it was the city, maybe it was what had built it, but it was there and he could not free himself of it.

He wasn't really worried about some nameless creature attacking them.

The Exosuits could withstand intense pressure and abuse and it would have taken quite a beastie to damage them. They were known as Atmospheric Diving Suits or ADS. They were self-contained and self-propelled, had pan-and-tilt video cameras, exterior halogen lights, color imaging sonar, and wireless radio connectivity through water. You could grasp and maneuver objects with robotic manipulators and move in any direction with vertical and horizontal thrusters. Out of the water, they were large, bulbous, and clunky like robots from an old Saturday afternoon serial. But in the water, they were something else. They could handle depths of 2000 feet while maintaining an internal pressure of one atmosphere. What that meant was that they eliminated the usual compression/decompression hazards of typical ambient pressure dives such as decompression sickness and nitrogen narcosis, a.k.a. *the bends*. This allowed the divers to enter and leave the habitat without hours of decompression. The life-support systems had air for eight hours and emergency support for forty-eight.

The suits were essentially anthropomorphic one-man robot submersibles. A suit of armor for the most extreme depths and conditions.

Yet, for all that hardware, Bell could not help feeling vulnerable like the suit was nothing but a tin can waiting to be crushed.

"Coming up on the vents," Murphy said.

A chasm opened up before them now, the SDV's lights picking it out foot by foot. There were dozens and dozens of tall, narrow chimney-like structures which were the remains of dormant hydrothermal smoker vents. They rose up fifty and sixty feet from the floor of the chasm, great craggy black spouts amongst which long, translucent, ribbon-shaped fish swam lazily like unfurled tapeworms. Being eyeless, the lights of the SDV had no effect on them. They were rather silly and harmless things that routinely bumped into the vents and each other. The SDV knocked a few aside and passed on, the vents climbing to all sides.

Bell found the place unpleasant, like some prehistoric cemetery of jutting monoliths.

But as eerie as they were, what came next was far worse.

12

THE CITY

Bell felt something in his stomach tighten like a screw. He could feel the city coming at them out of the gloom—its immensity and weight bearing down on him. Though he certainly could not smell it, in his mind it carried a vaporous, rotten odor like a violated tomb filled with moldering coffins. This was the effect its nearness had on him. A souring and rancid psychic effluvium that made his jaws lock tight.

And then…the outskirts, as revealed by the halogen lamps.

Rising from beds of yellow weeds and honeycombs of bryozoans were the outer ruins of the city: leaning, pitted rectangles and domes and massive slabs encrusted with corals and polyp colonies. And then more and more: jutting shafts like pointing fingers, worm-holed obelisks, pillars and multi-sided buildings that resembled ornate mortuaries. Everything was colossal, oversized, experiments in morbid gigantism and warped angles. Some of the pillars were hundreds of feet high, the rectangles like weathered blocks a giant had tired playing with.

The city rose up and spread out in every direction, as far as the lights could reach through those murky waters. Primeval ruins oozing with slime, draped with marine creepers and shrouded with colonies of bivalves and primitive corals. And the farther the SDV took them, the more complex and profuse the ruins became until it was a veritable necropolis of shattered pyramids, cracked domes, arches strung with deep-sea fungi, cones and monoliths, an elaborate system of multi-leveled barrow trenches intersecting them.

And by that point, Bell could feel his stomach actually pulsating with horror, jumping from all the adrenaline shooting through him in hot spurts. His chest was tight, his breathing coming fast, his heart rapping ceaselessly. The fear he felt of this place, the brooding genetic memory it inspired, was not just psychological or spiritual, but biological. He felt like he could have vomited out his intestines.

And then the ruins played out, fading into the murk, and here was the city proper.

Dear God, here it was as it had been for millions of years. The lights brought it into view through the raining silt and waving growths and once again, as always, he had to fight back a scream. The lights could only reveal the smallest portion of it, but that was plenty. It was black and stark, honeycombed and oddly machined in appearance. Something composed of a dozen geometrical shapes welded into a leaning, mushrooming whole.

He had seen the images taken of it by the hydrobot five years before and the video the ROVs and AUV Orca had sent back. He knew that it was a cyclopean, crumbling megalopolis, sepulchral and skeletal, rising up well over five-hundred feet from its mounded base to the very tops of its tomb yard expanse of spires and narrow pipes and spoke-like pinnacles. The AUV had confirmed that it was clustered over a series of rolling submarine mountains and covered an area of some three-square miles. Though in every direction, collapsed into hollows and nighted abysses, were ruins that spread out much farther. How large it had once been, was impossible to say now. Much of it was broken and crumbling like a megalithic fossil.

He could not get past the idea that, taken as a whole, the city looked almost like a castle...a very abstract, alien one as envisioned by ants or termites, but somehow castle-like. And he wondered if the castles men built were just embellished fortifications or if they were indeed inspired by race memories of places like this. Perhaps it was some unconscious attempt to duplicate the power of the alien cities, the grim and haunting majesty of them that would strike terror in the hearts of their enemies as these cities struck terror in the hearts of men.

As it was, Bell was glad he could not look up and see the thing rising above. What he could see...well that was more than enough.

Murphy brought the SDV to rest on a plate-like, fractured slab that might have been some sort of terrace once, but was now covered in corals and gorgonians. Worn, craggy sculptures like ornate headstones surrounded it in the pattern of five-pointed stars.

"I see you're on site," Javonivic's voice came over the comm and Bell jumped in his suit. "Watch yourselves. Keep in VR at all times."

"Yes, mother," Murphy said, trying damn hard to inject a little humor, even if his guts were knotted like string.

Bell said nothing.

What was there to say?

Today was the big day: the day Murph and he actually entered the city. They'd spent the last two days on recon, getting the lay of the land, so to speak, and now it was time. No more playing pretend, now it was time to enter the big bad spook house and see how that felt, what it did to them personally, psychologically, and, yes, physically. Time to see how many more scars they could slash and burn into the soft white underbelly of their souls.

Realistically, Bell knew, they could sit around and play dumb and tell themselves this was just another job, but that was bullshit. This was not just another job. Already what they had been through had wounded something in them that would never properly heal. If they lived to tell the tale, this lake, this fucking *city* would be with them for the rest of their lives, showing its malign face every time they closed their eyes and very often when they were wide awake.

That was the level of damage incurred.

Because this place inspired a devastating horror, both mental and physical, that was etched into the infancy of the race. It was in places like this that primitive men, and the distant ancestors of men, had interacted with the Elder Things, the bogies. And the memory of that was not only of extreme psychological duress, but of pain, physical pain, cutting agony.

And, good God, as he neared the structure itself, Bell could feel those memories. Physically feel them.

"You ready, Chief?" Murphy said.

Bell told him he was, leading the way in.

There were hundreds if not thousands of honeycombed entrances and he had chosen one pretty much at random. All of them were large enough to drive a truck into, or nearly, and one seemed as good as another for a cursory investigation within. Using the footpads inside the hardsuit, he activated the vertical thrust until he was up about twenty feet and at eye-level with the opening he wanted. Murphy hovered just behind him. Exterior suit lights cast a pool of illumination around him. He would not use his spots until he found something worthy of closer examination.

A slight tap of the horizontal thrusters and he entered the mouth of the tunnel that led into the belly of the city. It was perfectly circular, though it did not seem so with all the clustered growths of corals and carbonate skeletons of dead marine animals clinging to the walls like lumpy stucco. Green, slimy weeds grew up from the floor, swaying with a dreamlike motion from currents deep within. The suit halogens cast a swath of light for about twelve feet in front of him, but beyond that was an utter, colossal blackness. Clots of sediment slowly drifted about.

Ten feet in, he felt waves of anxiety wash through him. Looking at the city from outside was bad enough, but entering it unnerved him, made him feel somehow unclean. It was like sliding into the carcass of something long dead.

The weeds brushed against his suit with a dull rustling sound. The suit's sonar told him that the tunnel went on for about sixty feet. The water temperature was 38° Fahrenheit. There was a light current coming from ahead. Nothing in the tunnel, said the sonar, but themselves. Thirty feet into it, side passages opened up. Others went through the floor and still others through the ceiling. A labyrinth.

Murphy did not suggest going into them, but over the radio Bell said, "We stay on a straight course, make for that opening ahead."

"Roger that," Murphy said.

"What kind of magnetism we getting?"

Murphy had the magnetometer hooked to his suit. "Ah...holding steady at about one-ten. No increase yet."

Bell nodded inside his helmet. Something which was ridiculous since no one could see him. But like facial expressions, it was nearly impossible to get out of the habit.

Magnetism was measured in nanoteslas. About 70,000 nT was average at Kharkov Station. But the anomaly routinely put out sometimes four or five times that amount. When it started going off the scale, they would be in the vicinity of the anomaly itself.

They pushed on through clouds of sediment, random passages cutting off to the left and right thick with pooling shadow, strange fluttering growths. Tiny white crabs crept along the walls over the skeletons of generations of their ancestors. They were eyeless, but had slender antennae that looked like soda straws. Now and again, Bell caught a glimpse of a bare section of the tunnel, that odd black quartz-like material it was made from. It was sometimes shiny, sometimes lusterless, but never completely smooth. It had that same texture to it with bumps and knobs and threads like it had been worked on a lathe.

"I'm not getting anything from the habitat," Murphy said.

Bell tried himself, but there was only static.

"Probably the increasing magnetism," he said. "And maybe whatever this structure is made of."

It sounded reasonable. The suits were sending out a homing signal to the habitat so they could be tracked regardless of where they were in the city. Not radio waves, but microwaves. Hopefully Javonivic was still reading those or she'd start to panic.

The tunnel came to an end and opened into some sort of chamber. The lights could barely penetrate the murk and suspended silt. Without a word, Bell led the way in there.

13
LITTLE SARAH

Murphy figured he was some kind of pretender. Had to be, because he had even fooled himself into believing this place was not getting to him. And that took a special gift, a special talent for self-deception. The place bothered him just like it bothered Bell and the others, but he had talked himself out of it. He told himself, and made himself believe, that there was no danger here. No reason to be afraid, no reason to fear for his life or sanity.

And, goddamn, if it hadn't almost worked.

Funny how the human mind could totally fool itself. You could convince yourself that fire would not burn you when you touched a hot coal or a live 440 line would not fry your ass if you grabbed it or that in war you would not die in the dirt with your guts shot out. But, sooner or later, he knew, cold, ugly realization dawned and then look out. Because when the self-imposed delusions faded and the blinders were off and that creaking door of true perception was thrown wide, you were going to see things the way they really were.

And suffer for it.

Yes, the self-deception had worked.

At least while they were in the tunnel, but now, out here, in this impossible cloying pocket of darkness…his delusion of safety had failed. Completely failed. He was shaking, sweating, his heart pounding. His throat felt so tight he could not even speak. There was a lethal, dire magnetism to this place that had nothing to do with nanoteslas. This was a different wavelength, something older and infinitely more powerful that he could feel pulsating in the nerve ganglia of his spine like high voltage. It was real and electric and he could not deny it.

Come on, goddammit! Don't fold up now! You can't fold up now!

And he couldn't.

He knew he couldn't.

Bell was counting on him. He counted on all of them, just as Orr did, but he counted on him just a little bit more because Murphy was second-in-command. That and the fact they'd been diving with the DSU together now for something like fifteen years. Bell counted on him. And he counted on Bell.

But, damn thing was, whatever nerve he'd had was gone now.

He was hanging there, at the edge of the tunnel's mouth, and he had simply frozen up. Maybe it was this whole damn op and this fucking city in general, but maybe it was something more. Maybe it was what was waiting out there for them, because he had the strangest feeling that something was. Staring out through the face shield of his helmet, he was likening the darkness out there to the sort you'd find at the bottom of a grave or inside a coffin after the lid had been nailed shut on you.

He kept swallowing, but there was absolutely no spit in his mouth.

Bell was about five feet away, hovering like a buoyant shrimp, waiting. The lights from his suit cast twin beams that turned the water an amber color. They were filled with whirling sediment.

"Murph...you okay?"

He worked his mouth loose, found his voice. "Yeah...just taking it all in."

He steeled himself, knowing he had to dispense with the jitters, lock those ancestral fears down somewhere deep where they could not harm him or threaten the mission at hand. He'd done it before. So even with his insides knotted tighter than Aunt Tilly's corset, he pressed the footpads of the suit and went out there and right away, that electricity at his spine simply jolted him and his whole body seized up.

"Murph," Bell said over the headset, "something bugging you?"

Murphy coughed the flaking dryness from his throat. "Just…just had the funniest feeling that coming out here was like sticking my pee-pee in a hole where it did not belong."

"I got it, too. Let's just do this together. Sonar's saying this chamber is oval in shape, pretty damn big. It drops down one-hundred-fifty feet below us and shoots up another two hundred. Let's get the lay of it, look around, take some readings. Then we'll get the hell out of Dodge."

Murphy relaxed a bit.

The sound of Bell's voice reminded him that he was not alone.

They followed the curving wall for some time until they came back to the tunnel mouth. The chamber was roughly 300 feet in diameter, resembling a huge shaft or chimney. Like the outside of the city, the walls both above and below were honeycombed. But these were not entrances, but oval cells, about eight feet in diameter. Perfect size for one of the bogies, they both realized, but did not mention the fact. They examined about fifteen or twenty of them and there was nothing in them but silt and marine growths. They were abandoned and had been for a long time.

They dropped down fifty feet, went up fifty more. There was nothing to see but those glossy black machined walls and the cells. Murphy didn't like the chambers in the least. They were like the hollows in the carapace of an insect.

Funny, the stuff you would start thinking about in a situation like this. The darkness. The claustrophobia. That palpable sense of menace. It stirred things up in him, made him remember forgotten childhood fears and secret, nameless terrors. He was suddenly a kid again, back in Haymarket, the little dead-end burg he'd grown up in Wisconsin. There had been a nice girl in his class named Sarah Burges and she disappeared on Halloween night when he was nine-years-old. They looked for her for weeks. The entire town was in an uproar. People were fearing for the worst, that some child molester was on the prowl.

The sheriff enacted an after-dark curfew and had cars out all night long, shining spotlights in vacant lots and alleys and deserted playgrounds. The atmosphere in Haymarket was tense and scary. Then they dragged a local quarry and discovered her body. They said she must have fallen in. There were no signs of foul play or molestation.

Murphy had been terrified by it all, as a lot of kids were. Rumors ran wild that she was thrown in there—what the hell would she have been doing out at a quarry outside town when she was walking home from a Halloween party? But nothing was ever proven. The curfew remained in effect for weeks. He remembered lying in bed at night, imagining her down at the bottom of the quarry in her ragged, graying nurse's costume, her face puckered, slimy things crawling over her, her mouth packed with dead leaves and mud.

Why the hell am I thinking about that? he wondered. *Here. Of all places. I haven't thought about that shit in twenty years.*

"Hey, Murph? You with me?"

Murphy swallowed. It felt like his throat was full of grit. "You bet, Chief."

"Let's go down a little more," Bell said. "I want to see what's down there."

So they drifted down and down until they came to a floor of sorts. Of course, it was littered with debris and wavering lake weeds. But floor it was. Nearly, level. There was another passage down there winding into utter blackness.

The magnetometer started jumping right away.

"One-fifty," Murphy said over the intercom. Using his thrusters, he guided his Exosuit to the passage mouth. "One-seventy, one-eighty. Two hundred and holding steady. I bet it's going to keep rising in that tunnel, Chief. Should we...?"

"Negative on that," Bell said. "Not this trip. We've mapped out a route that'll get us closer to the anomaly. That's what we came to do."

They started up again and then they both stopped, canceling thrusters. They began to slowly sink back to the floor of the chamber.

"Sonar," Bell said. "You getting it?"

"Yeah."

They were not alone in the chamber now. Something was up there and it was coming down. It was big, according to the sonar imaging, about forty-feet long. Whatever it was, it was warm and alive. And it seemed to have come out of nowhere.

"Let's get back to the tunnel, Chief."

"No," Bell said, "we'd never make it. It's coming too fast. It'll be on us before we get there."

Murphy knew he was right, but the fear rising in him demanded he do something. He didn't want to wait here and—

"Stay put," Bell said. "Stand by with your spots. When it gets within thirty feet, put your lights on it."

"Fifty feet and closing," Murphy said, the lights of his suit filled with swirling specks of debris.

And what was really bothering him at that moment (besides the obvious), was that they had no weapons. The suits were tough. They could withstand just about anything. But to wait there with nothing to strike back with. It did not sit well with the human animal.

"A fish?" Murphy said.

"No…not swimming like that."

"Forty feet."

"Stand by with your spots."

"Thirty feet," Murphy said, his breath not wanting to come.

"Now!"

They activated their spots which illuminated a field above to well over twenty-five feet. When there was no light, even a little seemed like a lot. The spots didn't exactly turn night to day, but they certainly brightened things up. All that silt and sediment, tiny organisms darting about. And—

"Hell is that?" Bell said.

Murphy saw an immense, writhing shadow moving in his direction. It seemed to shimmer and sparkle, swimming side-to-side like a sea snake. But it was no snake and it was no worm. Just something worm-shaped that was composed of hundreds, thousands, of prismatic bubbles. Some were tiny, others bigger than softballs. They were indigo and orange and scarlet and deep green, purple and fiery red. Like the threads of a fiber-optic lamp, they kept changing color, lighting up like Christmas bulbs. Great bright bands of color ran lengthwise down the beast.

It was weird.

It was beautiful.

It was terrifying.

And then it stopped. The entire thing went a pulsing orange-red...and broke apart into separate bubbles that spread out in every direction.

"Jellies," Bell said over the comm from some distant place. *"Hydrozoans. Some kind of strange colony."*

Murphy knew about colonies of jellies. He'd been diving since he was sixteen-years-old. Colonies formed for a reason, but they did not mimic some huge creature. At least, not the kind he was familiar with. These had been acting in concert, pretending to be something else. Something big. Animals, both marine and terrestrial, often mimicked predators, but not in this way. This was amazing, alien, freakish even. Maybe a biologist who was particularly creative could have couched this in jargon that somehow made sense, toned it down and gave it a good whitewashing of logic... but Murphy was no biologist. He was a sailor. A diver. And he trusted his instincts. And they told him this was not just strange, but absolutely abnormal.

Hovering up there, the jellies certainly looked like your average jellyfish: they pulsed and oscillated, there were fine combs at their outer edges that jellies generally propelled themselves with. They did not look dangerous. They just hung there, perhaps attracted by the lights. They wouldn't have eyes as such, Murphy knew, but many jellies had photophores. The same light shows that attracted them to one another were attracting them to the divers.

"Just jellies," Bell said, as if he was trying to convince himself of the fact.

Murphy stared up at them. He couldn't seem to stop. There was something mesmerizing about them, captivating. It was almost like they wanted him to look at them and that was ridiculous, but the feeling persisted. Grew stronger, even.

"They're...they're dropping down now," Bell said, concerned, but certainly not frightened.

Not like Murphy was now.

Because as they started dropping like balloons at midnight on New Year's Eve—or, and more appropriately for his turn of mind, like spiders from some webby crawl space overhang-he suddenly felt about three inches from full-blown hysteria. They were descending and he could almost hear the slithery sounds they made, the rush of cold fluid in their bellies, the whickering of frill-like combs. His head pounded. He felt faint. The world spun and lilted. His heart hammered five or six times with an agony in his chest...and then it just stopped dead the way the venom of box-jellies would make it stop. He gasped and it started again, pounding so fast that the throb in his temples was like a drum roll, bringing a violent headache with it. His skin was damp and hot and constricted.

Bell might have said something; he wasn't sure really.

Because by then, he saw something like a whirlpool opening before him, spinning round and round, an agitated storm of bubbles reaching out toward him. He watched it with hypnotic fascination and it was as if his mind was rotating with it, a tornado of thoughts and impulses and cold fear.

And then the jellies were no longer jellies, but ...*faces*. White, pulsating faces with gigantic suckering mouths like those of sea lamprey. As terror flooded him in hot waves, he knew they had all become the face of Sarah Burges. The way his young mind had pictured it rotting away at the bottom of the quarry. Her eyes were black holes, her hair like squirming red worms.

The hungry faces filled his helmet view plate.

He thrashed the arms of the hardsuit around, the hydraulic rotary joints hissing as he moved them up and down and side to side. They did not move as fast as his arms wanted them to. In the hand pods, his fingers worked manipulators, trying to slash and cut the faces away from the suit.

He had never known such utter manic claustrophobia before as they made him part of the colony of corpse faces, enveloping him, suctioning leech mouths pressed up against the view plate.

They'll break through, they'll break through and get those mouths on me and suck the flesh from my bones, worry it away with those busy, chewing teeth. Help me, Bell! Jesus Christ, help me! They're squeezing me, squashing me! I can't breathe! I can't breathe! I can't fucking BREATHE—

Murphy fought and flailed, screaming in his helmet, but he never ever heard himself do so. The faces pulled away, dissolved in a gray, inky cloud and he saw something gigantic coming at him like a boiling, spinning whirlpool of sediment and black shadows...and reaching from it, three or four coiling, corpse-white tentacles, their undersides pink and bulging with suckers the size of teacups, a huge arching hook extending from each like the claw of a hunting cat.

He screamed again and the thing was gone, an expanding cloud of dark fluid in its place that engulfed him completely. His lights could only penetrate a few inches into it. It was opaque and whirling around him with cyclonic force. The terror inside him spiked, overwhelming him, shutting him down on just about every level. He tried to jet free from it, but it held him in a dark, muddy stasis and there was no escaping it. His neurons were misfiring, his limbs quaking, his mind filled with horrible images—

14
BREAKDOWN

It took Bell a few minutes to clear the jellies away with the plodding, mechanical manipulators of the hand pods. But he did it. When he started waving them off, most all of them darted away except the ones that had attached themselves to Murphy's suit for reasons he could not explain. They had been more tenacious. He killed dozens, their soft bodies rupturing beneath the metal manipulators, bursting into clouds of slime, rubbery shells floating about like used condoms. When he had peeled them off the view shield, he got a good look at Murphy—his face pale and sweaty, eyes staring. He looked to be in shock.

"Let's get the hell out of here," Bell told him, guiding him up to the tunnel and into its mouth.

Maybe five minutes into it, Murphy started coming around. "They were attacking me, Chief."

"No, Murph, they just got tangled on you or something."

"Don't give me that shit," he said, his voice breathless. "I saw it! They were faces and they had mouths!"

Bell said, "Murph, calm down. I tore them off you and they did not have mouths."

"They wanted to kill me," was all he would say.

Bell kept him moving, pressing deeper into the tunnel, desperate to get them on the SDV and back to the habitat. He didn't know how long they'd been out of contact with Javonivic.

They moved further and further through the tunnel, through the slime and silt, not talking, just fixed on what was ahead. And when the lights found the opening, Bell let out a sigh of relief because he had the funniest feeling that there would be no opening. Just a brick wall or something like there always was behind doors in haunted houses on TV.

But then they were out, dropping down towards the SDV, shadows swimming around the edges of their lights.

"I know you think I froze up, Chief," Murphy said when they finally got on the SDV. "I know you think I lost it in there, but you didn't see what I saw. Those things attacked. Do you hear me? *They attacked…*"

Bell didn't doubt it.

Not really.

This place wasn't right and you couldn't trust anything. He knew Murphy. He trusted Murphy. What he had seen was not what Bell himself had seen. Jellies did not attack. Bell had dived amongst colonies and schools before. Outside of a few dangerous species, they were harmless, amusing things. Even the ones that attacked did it out of simple stimulation, not rage or hunger. Jellyfish did not attack men. They just didn't. And those things had been jellies, strange and unknown types, but jellies all the same.

But what did that say? Murphy was hallucinating?

Yes, and no. The jellies wouldn't attack a man, not unless something directed them to, some force made them do it. The same force that made Murphy think they were monsters.

Mind games.

They had been in the city one hour exactly. And something had not wanted them there.

15

THE SCRATCHING

They were coming back now.

Thank God, they were coming back.

Bell had just radioed in that they were on their way.

Javonivic was sitting in the control room as she had been for hours, her face expressionless, her eyes just staring at the video monitors and the computer screen which fed her the telemetry from the hardsuits, giving her not only physiological factors such as the heart rate and oxygen usage of the divers, but water temperature and salinity etc. The numbers rolled in and she watched them, but her mind was in other places.

For something like an hour, while Bell and Murphy were in the city, there had been nothing coming in. No radio contact, no telemetry, no video images. Nothing. It was the city, Bell had told her when he came out. The city interfered with the signals. And that made perfect sense...yet, she was disturbed by it.

One hour, she thought as the divers were about thirty minutes from the habitat, plodding along in the SDV. *For one hour they were out of contact. One hour. Anything could have happened to them in that city. Anything.*

Yes, it bothered her.

It bothered her that all their high-tech, expensive technology and sensitive instrumentation had been blacked-out. And she knew why. She did not want to admit it, even to herself, but she was afraid that they had come into contact with something in there. It was pure human paranoia, but she couldn't stop thinking it.

She remembered what had happened at Kharkov Station five years before, how—supposedly—people there had stopped being people after awhile. How they had been something else, vessels for an ancient and diabolic evil. It had happened not just at Kharkov back then, but at the tent camp of the paleobiologist, Dr. Gates. She remembered the gossip about that. How Gates and his team had become infected by something while digging amongst the ruins of that city under the mountain. A city that sounded very much like what was at the bottom of Lake Vordog—

No, no, she couldn't afford this.

She would not allow herself to believe things unsubstantiated or be overcome by much-repeated urban legends. She simply could not afford such thinking. She put her face in her hands, fighting back the desire to openly weep. God, her nerves were shot, phobias and secret terrors blossoming inside her with wild abandon.

It's because you're a woman in a man's world, she heard the derisive voice of her mother say. *You're in a place you don't belong.*

"Shut up, Regina," she said under her breath.

But now that this place had resurrected the memory of the old bitch, Javy knew she'd never keep quiet.

And as she fought with her own painful memories in the silence of the habitat, Hubbs off doing whatever it was Hubbs did, she heard something that made her sit up straight.

Tense, her jaw locked tight, she listened again.

Yes, there it was.

A sort of scraping, scritching sound. The sound a spider might make against a windowpane. *That same sound you heard in your dreams, from inside your skull.* She did not like it. She suddenly felt very hot, very uncomfortable. A trickle of sweat ran down her back.

Licking her lips, she said, "Hubbs? Hubbs, is that you?" But she said it very quietly, as if she didn't want to be heard.

There was no reply, of course, and she hadn't expected one. Hubbs was not making the sound. He couldn't have been, because it wasn't coming from inside the habitat, but from *outside. Scratch, scratch, scrape, scratch.* It was too soon for the divers to be back. Which meant there was something else out there, something maybe trying to get in. Which would have been quite easy with the open moon pool.

Javonivic checked the sonar.

Nothing. She checked the outside motion detectors. Again, nothing. Something was making a sound, but it was motionless, insubstantial if the screens before her were to be believed.

She got out of her chair, touched the crucifix at her throat, waited for it to come again. It did. That same scraping, scratching noise that went right up her spine, made her think of insects, crickets maybe, rubbing their hind legs together. It was an invasive spiderlike sound that she found absolutely repelling. She wondered if it was the sound a fly heard as it lay paralyzed in the web of a garden spider, slowly being wound up in silk, those flat dead eyes looking at it, brown venom dripping from the monster's jaws.

"Stop it," she said under her breath. "Just stop it."

As a girl, she had been frightened of leggy and crawling things, and that scratching noise brought the memory of it back to her. Even as an adult, diving off Japan, she had been secretly revolted by spider crabs—so huge and leggy and weird. They were essentially harmless creatures and quite tasty dipped in butter…not that she could ever bring herself to eat something like that.

But it was the legs.

All those skittery, crawly legs. And what epitomized that terror for her were not crabs, but squids. It was a heck of a thing for a professional diver to be uneasy about, given that squid were one of the most abundant life-forms in the sea…yet, they got under her skin. As a child, she was fascinated by the various sea creatures trapped in tidal pools down at the shore. Whenever her mother was off running errands or at an appointment, she liked to wade into them (something she was absolutely forbidden to do by Regina; she wasn't allowed within twenty feet of the surf), investigating the myriad creatures—crabs and limpets, snails and mussels, sea stars and small fish.

One afternoon, there was a rare find: a short fin squid of about a foot in length. Sluggish and gray, she was certain it was nearly dead. Even when she gently poked it with a stick, it barely responded. After a time, she decided to pick it up for closer examination. And as she did so, bringing it up out of the water, it responded violently, squirting her with ink and chomping down on her thumb with its short, sharp beak. Screaming, she stumbled out of the water and ran home.

And there was Regina.

"What did I tell you about going into the water? What did I say to you?" her mother railed. "You got what you deserved and next time it will be worse." To emphasize this, Regina seized her bleeding thumb and squeezed it until Javy cried out. *"Stay out of the water! Do you hear me? Stay out of the damn water! Don't give them the opportunity they've been waiting for!"*

Even now, it made her thumb hurt.

"That miserable bitch," Javy grumbled.

The scraping came again and she knew it was coming from the viewport that looked out of the galley into the lake itself. She found her nerve and walked over there, down a short flight of steps from the control room. Her shoes rang out on the metal deck plates. She went in there wholly expecting to see a squid clinging to the glass, scraping at it with its beak, but there was no squid.

Something else.

Something that made her suck in a sharp breath and nearly fall over.

A shape.

She saw a dark shape move quickly away from the outside of the viewport. It had seen her. She knew it had seen her. For one microsecond, she saw red eyes looking at her…and then it was gone: something large and oblong-shaped fluttering away. Something with wings. She knew what it must have been. But it had not looked solid, just sort of filmy, insubstantial.

A ghost.

Jesus, it had been…a…ghost.

Javonivic stood there unsteadily, trying to wrap her brain around something that was in direct violation to everything that she believed in and held to be true. A ghost. A spook. Yes, there had been talk of such things at Kharkov five years ago, too. Ghosts of the Old Ones. Psychic emanations powered by human minds. Decayed intelligences that had never truly died, not in the human sense of death.

"I don't believe in ghosts," she said.

"Well, I'm glad to hear that," a voice said.

She swung around and Hubbs was standing there, looking amused. He had always been the emotionless, cold type. He smiled rarely, emoted about as much as a marble bust. But lately, and particularly since they'd gotten down to the Neptune, he'd been acting spooky: smiling, acting like he knew something the others didn't. Some big secret he did not want to share.

"I...I didn't know you were there," Javonivic said, feeling more than a little foolish.

"You never struck me as the sort to talk to themselves."

"I'm not."

He smiled thinly. "Well, this place changes a lot of things, don't it?"

She sighed. "What's that suppose to mean?"

"You tell me." He walked over to the viewport, staring out into the murky depths illuminated by the exterior habitat lights. Tiny swimming forms darted about. "What did you see out there, Javy?"

"Nothing."

"Bullshit. You saw something. Don't worry, I won't tell anyone. I know what it's like to see things."

She turned away, headed back up to the control room and Hubbs followed her as she knew he would and hoped he wouldn't.

"It's the shits, ain't it, Javy?" he said as she studied the telemetry from the Exosuits. "When everything you know or thought you knew turns out to be wrong. It's just the absolute shits. You come down here not believing in things like ghosts and spooks and aliens...or telling yourself that you don't...and then it all changes. One day you're sweet little Pollyanna Javonivic, saying your prayers and watching over the team like little Mother Hubbard and the next? The *next*, Pollyanna dies a really ugly death when she realizes the world ain't what she thought it was. Just like the human race ain't what she thought it was. It's hard. It's just the absolute shits."

She ignored him. It was his usual nihilism, his typical need to stomp on other people's beliefs. Only down here, he was even more negative, pessimistic, and vocal about it. She would not discuss it or turn this into another debate. It was pointless.

Of course, having dropped his pearl of observational wisdom for the day, he still would not go away. He stood there staring at her with the brown, glassy eyes of a stuffed moose. She saw no true intelligence in them and certainly no compassion. Yet, they fixed her, drew her in, and there was a sudden, inexplicable crackling noise in her head that reminded her vaguely of static electricity. Her vision blurred. Her head swam with vertigo. She heard that scraping/scratching sound in her skull again, like a worm chewing its way free of a seed. *I know what you saw. I know what you're hiding. I know what terrifies you, little boy.* The voice speaking in her head made her cringe. For a moment, she thought she was reading his mind, conceptualizing his thoughts...but, no, it was something else. Not his voice. Not her own. But one that sounded unpleasantly like that of her mother. *He can't hide his little boy sissy fears from us.* And Javy nearly screamed...but she *saw.* Oh yes, indeedy, she actually saw his fear—the horrible eye he had seen through the viewport that day and...and...and in the city, something else: an immense, grotesque creature with dozens of wavering white legs.

Like a squid, a monstrous squid.

Then whatever connection there was dissipated, her mind filled with confusing, conflicted images.

Hubbs kept staring at her, then he said, "You should have listened to your mother."

Javy felt her face go red as a beet. *"What did you say? What the fuck did you just say?"*

That quick she was on him, grabbing hold of him, ready to swing.

"Javy," he said in a soft voice. "I didn't say anything. I didn't even open my mouth."

It felt like the air was bled from her. She felt weak, limp as a rag. *He didn't say it, you idiot, he thought it.* She wrapped her arms around herself, embarrassed, self-conscious, ashamed. "I...I thought..."

"It's okay, Javy. I understand. I know how crowded it gets in your head sometimes. Oh, I know."

They waited there in silence, watching the board. The tension between them gradually faded. Finally, he said, "How long, Javy? How long were they in the city?"

"An hour."

"No contact for an hour, eh?"

"No."

"Lots of things could happen in an hour. Especially in that fucking graveyard."

Javonivic reeled out the reasons why the technology had failed. The city. It was the city itself. What it was made of and the intense magnetic field emanating from it. The water would dampen that somewhat, but inside it would be much more intense.

Hubbs nodded. "Could be that. Could be something else."

"Meaning?"

"Meaning, maybe they came into contact with something in there."

God, her own paranoia spoken aloud. But she had already dismissed that, would not even consider it.

"That's ridiculous, Hubbs."

"Is it? Things happened at Kharkov last time, you know. Maybe they're happening again. Every time we go into that city, Javy, a little bit less of us comes out."

"You're being paranoid."

"Yes, I am, Javy. And you should be, too. Because things are not what they seem down here and you shouldn't be inclined to believe everything your eyes show you or take things at face value. Things are going to happen to us. And I just have to wonder if any of us will make it topside again."

Javonivic tried her best to ignore him. He was becoming increasingly unstable. The sonar started to beep. "The SDV's coming in. Bell and Murphy are coming back."

"Are they?" Hubbs said.

"Goddammit, Hubbs! Knock it off. I don't need this nonsense. Get to the moon pool. They'll be coming up in about ten minutes."

But he shook his head. "You go, Pollyanna. I'm not so sure I want to see what comes up out of that pool."

16
TALES TOLD

Later, after they were back in the habitat, warm and fed, away from the others, Bell said, "Tell me what happened. I need to know."

Murphy thought of dozens of ways he could lie about it, his well-tuned DSU ego demanding he save face, but in the end, he told the truth. What he knew of it. What he could remember. He told Bell about the whirlpool and how everything had gotten weird after that.

"It was the weirdest thing I've ever seen. Even now, I can't make sense of it."

"I didn't see anything like that," Bell told him.

Murphy swallowed. "I saw it. I know I saw it."

"And then?"

"The jellies...they just attacked me. It was insane." He breathed slowly for a moment or two. "You know me, Chief. You know how I am. I don't panic. I barely break a sweat. But..."

"Go ahead, tell me."

It took Murphy a few minutes to get it out. What he had to tell was not something a man in his line of work liked to admit. "I was scared, Chief. I mean I was *really* fucking scared. I'd never felt anything like that before. I've been deep in the shit dozens of times and you know it...but this...it was...I don't know, but like whatever controls fear inside me was jacked to the limit, amplified, right off the scale." He sipped water from a bottle and his hand shook. The memory of what he'd experienced made his lips pull into a tight gray line. Tiny beads of sweat speckled his brow. "You hear people say they were paralyzed with fear and that's exactly how it was. I couldn't think. I couldn't move."

Bell considered it. "And this happened right after the whirlpool?"

"Yes. At that very moment." Murphy breathed deeply, trying to calm himself. The memory still had power over him. "There's more to it than that. I mean, shit, Chief, I hate to even tell you."

"Tell me. It stays between us."

It took Murphy some time, but he did. He told Bell about the faces, that looked suspiciously—and frighteningly—like that of Sarah Burges… the way he had imagined she'd looked down in the quarry when he was a kid: bloated, rotting, fish-nibbled. "That's the craziest part. Soon as we got into the city, I felt…I don't know…*uneasy,* I guess, which is understandable. But it was more than that. My fear kept amping up, getting stronger and stronger. For some reason, I was thinking about Sarah ten, fifteen minutes before it happened. It came back to me. I mean *really* came back me. The way all that felt when I was a kid. The way it scared the shit out of me."

Bell thought it over for a time. "What bothers me, Murph, is that it was on your mind. Then it on physical form. That really disturbs me."

"Yeah, me, too. It was like the thing that scared me most as a kid was plucked from my mind. Crazy." He sighed slowly. "Is it possible that us entering the city triggered something?"

Bell shrugged. "Could be. We're dealing with a technology beyond anything we know. Anything's possible."

Neither of them spoke for a time. Murphy knew himself as well as any man does and maybe even better because of the intensive psych profiling that had been done on him because of his dangerous occupation. He knew exactly how his mind worked. Fear did not break him. He felt it like anyone else, but he was cool by nature. He did not panic and he sure as hell did not freeze up.

"When you were pulling the jellies off me, it happened again."

"You screamed, Murph," Bell said. "I've never heard anyone scream like that in my life."

"The faces, they sort of dissolved away into a dark cloud and I saw something…something coming out of it."

"What?"

"Tentacles…but like none I've ever seen before. They had claws on them the way Colossal Squid do, sharp hooks."

"You think it was a squid? In fresh water?"

Murph shook his head. "No, Chief, I don't."

"Then what?"

He explained that he'd only seen the tentacles for a moment. What they were attached to he couldn't even guess. But since he'd gone that far, he went further. "Squid don't scare me, Chief. I've seen some big ones on dives, everything from Magnapinnas to Giants. I was attacked by a school of Humboldts off Baja one time on a wetsuit dive. They went after me like I was wrapped in fucking bacon. By the time the other divers got me up, I needed forty stitches to stop the bleeding." He shook his head. "No, this was no squid…not the kind we know anyway. I think it lives in the city. If you hadn't been there, it would have gotten me."

Bell was disturbed by the very idea. That much was obvious. "Let's keep this to ourselves for now. I'll let Orr know, but I don't want Javy and particularly Hubbs getting wind of this."

Bell was worried about Hubbs because he knew he'd seen something in the city. Something bad. He told Murph that he couldn't get him to admit what it was. No amount of threatening could get him talking.

"Hell, I even told him I'd bust him out of the DSU. No dice. He won't say a word."

Murph nodded. "Sure, I get that, Chief. But if they're going in there and that thing is in there, maybe they need to know."

"Not just yet. You leave it to me."

Murph didn't like it, but Bell was in charge, so that's how it had to be.

17
THE THING IN THE CORNER

That night, or what passed for night down in the habitat, Javonivic lay in her bed, eyes wide open. She was afraid to sleep. Each time she closed her eyes, it was as if her head became some kind of receiver and she picked up broadcasts from the city. They reverberated in her brain. Buzzing, droning sounds that she knew were the voices of the Old Ones calling to her, summoning her to join them in the black depths of the ruins where they would show her things, wonders beyond anything she could image.

They did not come in words exactly, but as distorted images, one after the other after the other until she thought she would scream. Several times, she nearly got up and went to Bell to tell him that she was losing her mind or having a nervous breakdown, and she needed to get to the surface before her head blew apart.

But she never did.

She was a DSU diver. She was made of sterner stuff. If she gave into weakness or, God help her, admitted the same out loud, she was finished. She might still be in the DSU, but in a support position.

"I won't," she whispered to herself in the darkness. "I will not give in."

Yes, you will, Regina's shrewish voice told her. *You'll give in like the silly little girl you are, Alice. And when you do, it'll be worse than anything you can imagine.*

Javy felt herself burn with anger, with outrage, with a curious, unsettling combination of terror and rage. In the depths of her mind, she shouted, *GO AWAY! GO AWAY, YOU NASTY FUCKING BITCH! LEAVE ME ALONE! DO YOU HEAR ME? LEAVE ME THE FUCK ALONE!* But even as the words echoed with a grim finality in her mind, she knew that the attempted exorcism had been a glaring failure. Regina would not go away. So many, many years ago, she had locked the memory of her mother in the darkest trunk she could find and wound in chains. It had been sunk into the deepest, darkest pit of her psyche. But now…here in this place, at the very bottom of the world at the very bottom of this damned lake, the trunk had resurfaced, the chains and lock rusted away, and Regina had sprung out of it like a Jack-in-the-box, like a grinning Halloween skeleton from a coffin.

And I'll never go away, you stupid girl. Never. Ever. Ever.

As she hovered at the outer edge of a troubled, tormented sleep, Javy's mind went back again to her childhood.

Many months after Regina had disappeared, Javy had an episode in school that she had tried unsuccessfully to forget about. For weeks, she had been unable to sleep much. What there was of it was haunted by nightmares of her mother that she would wake from, sweating and shivering. She was worn out, both physically and mentally. She was losing weight, seeing shapes moving out of the corners of her eyes. Constantly haunted by the sense that she was never alone, that she was being watched and followed. It was a very bad time.

It all came to a sudden, screaming head in 3rd hour American Lit. She looked up from her textbook, her exhausted brain reeling as it tried to take in Thoreau's life of seclusion at Walden's Pond, and there was a shape standing in the corner.

It leered at her.

It chattered its teeth.

It grinned like a man-eating shark.

At some point, Javy had screamed, then passed out cold. She came to sometime later in the office of the school nurse, who managed to pry from her the fact that she had not eaten in nearly four days. She did not admit that she couldn't eat because everything tasted like rank seawater or that she had clearly seen Regina standing in the corner. But not a living Regina, of course, but a Regina who had been sunk in the mud and slimy green weeds at the bottom of the bay, a grotesque barnacle-encrusted horror chewed by fish and crabs, her eye sockets crawling with brine shrimp, her tongue replaced by a bloated green sea worm that licked her lips.

Javy had clearly heard the sound of water dripping from the apparition and striking the floor.

But she couldn't admit to any of that.

Aunt Ida had fed her soup and watched her constantly after that. And, thankfully, the episode had never repeated itself. Somehow, Regina had slowly faded from her mind and her dreams.

And now she was back.

But why?

Why?

She could hear Regina cackling in her mind. *All will become apparent,* she said. *Because in the end, they always come for their own.*

Javy laid there, shaking, knowing that somehow, the old bitch was right. Tomorrow, she was scheduled to go into the city with Hubbs and it was going to be bad. In fact, she was quite sure it would be a nightmare.

18
LITTLE LOST GIRL

In her hardsuit, she could hear Orr's voice echoing out with a shrill, insectile whine: *"Javy? Goddammit, Javy...where are you? Talk to me!"* She moved through the tunnel, her suit lights filled with swirling sediment and tiny swimming marine animals. She tried again and again to contact Orr or Bell in the Neptune, but they weren't receiving her. She could pick them up off and on, but not consistently. There was some kind of interference and the nature of it scared her.

They're toying with you and you know it. The masters of this city don't want you here, she thought, *so they're making you run the maze like a rat.*

She was panicking in the dark belly of the city. Nothing was making sense. She had been exploring a chamber with Hubbs and he had discovered another opening...and then, well, that's where things became not only murky, but twisted. He had been in VR, not more than eight feet from her, and then an immense shadow had passed between them and she had thought at the time, *Like a whale, like the shadow of a whale,* and then it was gone, but so was Hubbs.

Think, she kept telling herself the way her DSU instructors had told her. *Do not panic. Consider the situation. Adapt to it.*

Yes, but how was that possible? She was in a hostile alien environment. Anytime a diver went down in the deeps, he or she was, of course, but here in this awful place it was even more so. In the labyrinth of the city, she relied on the technology of her suit. But it wasn't behaving right. Hubbs' suit should have been sending out a homing beacon that she should have easily picked up, but it wasn't. She should have been able to send voice transmissions to the LSB and habitat, but she couldn't. And worse, oh yes, worst of all, the suit's mapping system should have led her back to the opening of the city, but it wasn't. It kept leading her to dead ends.

Were the others monitoring her?

Did they know where she was?

It seemed unlikely.

She was confused and turned around and Hubbs was nowhere to be found. It made no sense. At least, until you factored in the city itself. Then maybe it made all the sense in the world.

I will not cower in fear.

She realized she had been drifting there ten minutes or more, thinking, gathering wool, but not doing a damn thing to further her own escape. She stared dreamily at the walls of the tunnel, the skeletonized remains of barnacles, mussels, clams, and various bivalves that clung to it. The walls were lumpy with generations of their deposits.

Death, she thought. *The city is made of death.*

As if in evidence of this, a small white worm emerged from a chambered shell. It swam through the murky water, pausing inches from her face shield before swimming off.

A sharp burst of static came over her helmet comm and she let out a small, strangled cry. She waited for a voice transmission, but there was nothing but a low squealing, a few sonar-like pings, then silence.

"Bell," she said into the suit mic. "Chief, can you hear me? Orr? If you're getting any of this, I'm looking for Hubbs. We got separated...not sure how. I'll keep at it as long as I can." She waited, hoping they'd pick it up, but there was no reply coming in. Not so much as a peal of static. She might as well have been on the dark side of the moon. "Hubbs...Hubbs, if you're injured, activate your emergency beacon. I can track you with it."

Nothing.

She knew she had to keep her head screwed on straight or she was finished. She couldn't count on Bell or Murphy coming to her rescue; she had to effect it herself. She knew her life signs were all over the place. She kept imagining them like wild horses running to and fro, trying to bust free from a corral. She had to relax. The more worked up she got, the faster her heart would beat and the more oxygen she would burn.

She breathed slowly, deeply. Much as she hated the idea, it was pointless to try and find Hubbs. She couldn't track him which meant the only way she would find him was by stumbling over him, something which could conceivably take weeks in this mausoleum if not months.

Okay then. Survival.

Her onboard navigator beeped, telling her she was moving in the wrong direction if she wanted out. Which was crazy, because not ten minutes ago, it had pointed her this very way.

She didn't have time to think it over. She went back the way she came, moving back down the tunnel, her lights casting crawling shadows all around her. The tunnel split. Yes, she remembered that. The navigator indicated the right branch and she followed it along, moving slowly but steadily. She came to the end of it before long and its mouth was thick with some sort of slimy, wavering sea grass that almost looked like cilia.

The navigator wanted her to keep moving.

She exited the tunnel into another huge chamber, her lights filled with swirling sediment. A long, ropy creature like something made of silly string passed by her. She thought it might be a giant siphonophore, another deep-sea creature. Like many of the life-forms in Lake Vordog, it had no business being in a freshwater lake. But there it was.

The navigator said the tunnel mouth she wanted was down towards the bottom, so Javy let herself sink into the encompassing blackness. At the bottom, she found herself in a forest of gigantic tube worms that grew around her in great profusion. There had to be hundreds and hundreds of them. They were a bloodless white with pink frills at the tops where their mouths were. They moved sluggishly, rising easily four or five feet above her. As she pushed gently through them, she felt like a flea moving through a forest of follicles on a dog's back.

She knew she had never been in this place before.

The navigator was leading her in circles.

She was going to die down here.

You need to accept something, she told herself, refusing to lose her nerve.

All of this may be hallucination placed in your mind to break you with fear and paranoia. Maybe the bogies themselves are doing it and maybe it's this goddamn city itself.

She had to keep moving. That was imperative. She'd given up on the comm because all she was picking up now was static. The navigator assured her she was moving in the right direction. The tube worms brushed against her suit, bumping her view plate and sliding over her with vague rustling sounds. It was like being trapped in a crowded forest of dead trees that seemed to have no end, terrible and claustrophobic.

She realized she was smelling the depths of the city, even though that was patently impossible. But it filled her helmet—a smell of age, black mud, decay, and pervasive dankness. But there was something else, too, something just beneath all that—a hot, fusty animal smell like the stink of a wolf's den, a place strewn with bones and moldering scraps.

It's in your head, she kept telling herself. *You can't smell anything in the suit and you know it.*

Now the air seemed thin, metallic-smelling, poisoned. She began to gasp, panicking despite her iron nerve. The clustering tube worms were clutching at her, grasping her suit like fingers, tightening, pressing in. She felt like a fly trapped in the strands of a spider's web.

You have your faith. Remember that.

She worked the jets and drove through them like a bullet and she could hear them crying out in her head with a shrill squeaking sound that blotted out everything else. She cried out as their rubbery stalks pulled at her, snared her, trying to trap her.

And then she was free, her heart pounding, sweat running down her face. She whirled around with the jets and the forest of tube worms were motionless, eerie in their profusion, but utterly harmless.

Slowly, she brought her breathing down and turned toward the tunnel mouth. Except…suddenly, the mouth was replaced by whirling, churning suck hole. Her fear spiked and she began to pray in a desperate, whispering voice. Her entire body was shaking. She couldn't seem to move. Her head was filled with gurgling noises and slithery sounds. Unseen things brushed the suit, making scratching sounds against its shell.

What…

What the hell is...

What the hell is happening to me?

There was a surge of adrenaline inside her, an absolute eruption of it followed by a wild, hysterical, absolutely debilitating rush of pure, primal fear. It was uncaged and shrieking inside her, filling her mouth with white foam that bubbled down her chin as her lips trembled and her teeth chattered, her eyes wide and wet, her body quaking with terror.

Stark, berserk memories tangled in her brain and she saw Regina's hard, cruel face staring down at her, her teeth bared, her huge eyes glassy and round like those of a predatory fish. Her mother's sure, bony hand hardened by a lifetime of manual labor slapped her again and again and again until black constellations and imploding stars detonated in her head—

(you stupid stupid troublemaking little bitch i told you and told you not to go in the water never go in the water never swim in the sea and you broke my rules you broke them)

—and she cried, she screamed, but Regina kept hitting her and hitting her. Blood ran from her nose and split lip. She writhed and fought but Regina would not let go of her, would not let her fall to the floor.

(swimming with the boys you little slut disobeying me and swimming i warned you time and again what that dirty seawater would do to you)

And then Regina let her fall and she struck her head on the hardwood floor, but there was no pain because Regina kicked her again and again, stomping her. Finally, she grabbed Javy by her wet ponytail and dragged her across the room and right out the back door, throwing her in the grass.

(do you see it out there do you see it do you feel its pull drawing you into green depths that you can never escape you little witch you awful awful little witch)

Javy, battered and bleeding, saw the sea, yes, the setting sun making the dark waters glow red, but she didn't understand. It was just the sea, the ocean, that's all it was...just water, nothing but water. It couldn't hurt you.

Regina fell into the grass next to her, undergoing terrible muscular spasms and violent contractions that made her gasp and drool and roll in the grass like a poisoned dog.

And then the memory faded and Javy jetted forward, the whirlpool gone. She was in the tunnel and it canted wildly to the left and the right, widening, narrowing. She saw flickering light ahead that looked disturbingly like that of guttering candles. Then the tunnel opened into another chamber.

And what she saw in it was absolutely impossible.

19
BODIES

Terror that was both hot and cold filled Hubbs like pumped blood fills an artery. He was woozy and disoriented with it, childhood fears and adult anxieties splashing around in his head in conflicting currents. He waited there, drifting, floating, doubting what his eyes showed him, certain that he was lost in some hallucination. Maybe he wasn't even in the city. Maybe he was trapped in a nightmare that he could not wake from.

Yet, he kept thinking, *Bodies…oh Jesus, look at all those goddamn bodies.*

He was in an endless passage, a barrow tomb without end, and he thought maybe he'd always been in it, carried along like a speck of silt. As he was drawn deeper and deeper into it, he wondered vaguely if Javonivic was even still alive or if she had ever existed in the first place.

Inside his head, he could hear dozens of voices competing for his attention. Some of them were sobbing. Some were screaming. Others were laughing with a shrill, insane sound. The cacophony of the damned went on and on.

The tunnel was made of bodies.

They were faintly luminous like noctilucae.

They grew in and out of the walls in a deranged, pulsating anatomical puzzle, something that was part machine and part living tissue, a terrible excrescence of fleshy hoses and bone pipes and convoluted networks of tissue and gears and ribbed projections, jutting bones and limbs and agonized faces with hollow-socketed eyes. A nightmare, industrialized fusion welded into a common whole, horribly alive and functioning in some dire symbiosis. Faces were distorted into screaming fright masks, huge crater-like carbuncles giving birth to coiling arrow worms and the fluttering tentacles of anemones. Sea lice crawled in drifting kelp-like mops of hair, bodies rife with barnacles and mussels like the hulls of sunken ships.

Everything seemed to slowly pulsate and crawl, vibrate and tremble with a horrendous rhythm.

Hubbs heard a wild, shrieking cry like that of a hyena and he realized it was coming from inside his own head. He tried to blink away what he was seeing, but its reality was unimpeachable. The tunnel was a great, corkscrewing biomechanical machine, empty eyes creeping with tiny crustaceans staring out at him, hundreds of mouths opening and closing like those of deep-sea fish.

No, no, no…I don't want this. Please let me go…just let…me…go.

He was being pulled deeper and deeper into it. His Exosuit would not respond. The controls were dead. The city wanted him to become part of it and he could feel that to his core. What he was seeing was secret and ancient and unknown. The desire to be part of it surged inside him.

As the laughter of the many mouths continued to echo in his skull, he realized how easy it would be. All he had to do was activate the emergency release and jettison the suit and he would be free, a shining pearl ejected from an oyster, a baby bird bursting from an egg. *Yes, yes, yes!* the voices cried. They screeched like rusty hinges and crackled like static discharges until he could not think rationally.

Yet, through the chaotic, incomprehensible babble of voices and the forking lightning of impulse and the ice-cold implosions of fear in his chest and belly, his own voice called out, *No, you fucking idiot! If you release the suit you'll die! You'll drown! Suffocate!* And as he thought that, he realized that something was happening inside the suit…he was being colonized. Crawling, dripping things like weeds and sponges, sea cucumbers and plaits of red algae were consuming him. They were dissolving his flesh, adhering to his skeleton, burrowing and infesting and if he didn't jettison the suit, there would be nothing left of him.

All the faces called to him, offering him a release of purity. All he had to do was get free of the suit and then he could join them, be linked with them, another cog of the great synergistic machine that throbbed in his ears with unbelievable motive power. He could feel its psychic force drilling into him, shattering his skull into pieces, macerating his brain.

(Hubbs Hubbs Hubbs)

(be with us as us)

(be part of the machine)

(another cell in its body)

He recoiled from the voices. He would not listen. They wanted him to kill himself, to offer himself as sacrifice, prostrate before the great beating heart of the machine. It lusted for his suicide. It needed him. He was the fuel it needed to burn, but he wouldn't allow it. He was going to escape; he was going to get out of this awful place.

Although he was terrified and confused, he felt strength inside him and he knew it would deliver him if only he focused on it. He had to concentrate. Remember his training. Mine his experience. The city was alive around him. It was trying to contaminate him, infest him with its creeping foulness. He had to fight it with everything he had or he would become part of it, just another screaming voice, another tormented soul being leeched slowly dry, a parasitized carcass fused to it that kept its diseased, alien heart beating.

The clarity in his head came in brief flashes and spurts of purity, hosing away the accumulated detritus the city was trying to drown him in. And as it did, he could no longer feel things crawling in his suit, colonizing him like he was a sunken ship.

He could be free if he indeed *wanted* to be free.

(NO NO NO NO DO NOT PULL AWAY DO NOT REJECT WHAT IS OFFERED)

The Exosuit began to react now that he fought against the city and its attendant systems. Slowly, slowly, it began to pull back toward freedom, toward deliverance. He could feel the rage of the countless minds that made up the whole. They were angry, screeching, offended at his defiance. The city would not have it. He could feel the minds telling him that. There would be punishment.

Then it took form.

It was coming down the tunnel to the chorus of screaming voices—a bloated, misshapen vermiform creature easily eight or ten feet in length. It was white and spongy like the flesh of a mushroom with a snaking, eel-like body that was shivering and gelatinous with a great spiny, central fin running down its back. It had no recognizable head as such, but the fore end terminated with a flabby, suctioning mouth from which stout, coiling tentacles emerged, each terminating in a puckering, toothed orifice. Tiny white threads and fibers floated around it like the albumin of eggs, creating a slimy, jiggling envelope that reminded him of an embryonic sac.

A mad rush of terror spread through him and he had to choke back a scream. *It's the city,* he told himself again and again. *The city is manufacturing this, trying to break you with fear.* But that did little to calm him. As it swam in his direction, it paused now and again, a smooth and slender mosquito-like proboscis jutting from its mouth and suctioning to one agonized face after another, seeming to drink from them, perhaps tapping into the raw psionic juice of their minds.

Hubbs kept trying to pull back, but everything was weird and dreamlike and he barely moved inches as it closed the gap. Then with the speed of a striking moray eel, it was on him, winding its body around his suit, exerting enormous pressure. His Exosuit began to groan as its integrity was tested. Warning lights flashed inside. He began to grow very warm, sweat running down his face.

The city could not convince him to leave the suit willingly, so the creature would crush him inside it, squeeze him out of it like toothpaste from a tube.

Its mouth sucked at the face bubble, the tentacles exploring every seam and joint, looking for a way in. By that point, Hubbs was hysterical with fright. He couldn't seem to get his racing imagination under control.

And then, quite suddenly, he didn't want to.

He wanted to be free from the cage of his suit. He wanted to be embraced by this horror. He wanted to be sucked into its gelid membrane and have his mind vacuumed from his skull so that he could be part of something much larger.

My God, that was not only necessary.

It was imperative.

As insane as it seemed, his body was burning hot with desire. He wanted the creature to touch him, to embrace him, to slide its proboscis inside him and drain him dry. Trapped in the suit, he was like a man overcome with lust that couldn't peel himself free of his clothes as a beautiful, exotic woman spread her long limbs for him.

He had to make contact with it.

He had to become part of it.

He hungered for the union.

Then, as his desire neared completion, a voice in his head—one well-disciplined by rigorous, demanding training—simply said, *no.* It stopped him. It shocked him out of it. As the creature enveloped him in slime, winding itself around him in loathsome coils, the voice of his well ingrained survival instinct slapped him out of it. *All you have is your life. Fight for it. Fight now.* The controls obeyed. He lifted one of the arms and it broke free of the creature, the claw-like manipulator on the hand pod seizing one of the tentacles and snipping it in half like scissors.

The creature went wild, exuding a foaming blue-black cloud of blood like the ink of a squid. It pulled away as the manipulator cut channels into it.

Hubbs turned the suit around and jetted down the tunnel, the inside of his skull filled with the screaming essences of those trapped by the machine.

20
A MOTHER'S SECRETS

Though it was absolutely impossible, Regina was waiting for Javy in the chamber. And though it was also not possible that she could speak underwater (or that Javy could even hear her), she said, "It's about time you came home, Alice."

A surreal, hallucinatory sense of wavering reality filled Javy's head. The real world could no longer hold its shape. "Tell me," she said. "Tell me what you've always wanted to tell me. There's always been a secret. I could see it in your eyes."

Regina ignored that, simply shaking her head the way she'd always shaken her head at her daughter, as if everything she said were the ramblings of a congenital idiot.

Using the jets of her suit, Javy moved further into the chamber which had now become the living room of the house she had grown up in. The drab, ugly green carpet had become seaweed now, emerald and yellow and slimy, yet luxuriant in its abundance, the individual fronds and blades moving back and forth as if caught in a secret tidal pull. Corpse-white tube worms grew up from the algae-encrusted sofa. Clusters of clams and mussels covered the walls. Sea stars clung to the lampshades and pink-red marine growths dangled from the ceiling like Spanish Moss. Where the coffee table had been, there was the rotting husk of the rowboat Regina had disappeared in. Its hull was riven, crawling with tiny white crustaceans, groupings of brightly-colored brain coral growing inside it.

Regina's armchair was facing the TV as usual, though it was invisible beneath colonies of bubble-tipped anemone. Krill and sediment were suspended in Javy's light. Giant isopods roamed the floor.

"In the beginning," Regina said, "the Earth was without form, and void. When they came, when the Old Ones first arrived, they created life in the sea, they engineered the proto-shoggoth, the progenitor of all life on this planet. And at our very genetic core, its still waits, dreaming across countless ages."

"Mother, oh please, I don't know what you mean…"

Javy realized that she was sobbing. Inside her suit, encapsulated in it like a nucleus at the heart of a cell, she was whimpering like a little girl. Tears rolled down her face to her trembling lips and her scalp crawled with hot sweat. Oh God, she was alone, she was so very, very alone and she had been her entire life and this made her bray with half-choked sobs.

"You are a woman who has been given the gift, but spurns it," Regina went on. "You try to be a man when men are nothing but the purveyors of the seed. It is the woman that is life. It is the woman that is continuance. It is the woman that spawns life in these green depths. And you turn away from that most precious of gifts that was instilled, engineered into our kind."

"No, no, Mother. I'm more than that, I'm—"

"You are a breeder and that is your purpose. The reason you were given breath. To breed and multiply and fill the dark waters with your spawn. In the beginning, we came from the sea and in the end, we must return to it."

Inside the suit, Javy shook her head from side to side because this was all blasphemy in accordance with her beliefs. As Regina continued to speak of life on Earth and how humans were engineered from wild beasts, intelligence instilled within us, a crop the aliens had sown and would now reap in a final, diabolical harvest, Javy felt like she could not breathe. She felt Regina's knobby, callused hands squeezing the life out of her.

"You will take your place amongst our kind and fulfill your destiny."

Javy trembled with fear and rage, with repulsion and anger. Her entire life, this woman had tormented her, squashed her, made her feel small and weak and meaningless. She had sucked the blood from her veins and drawn the air from her lungs. She had stepped on her again and again like a squirming bug. Even in death, it hadn't stopped. The evil hag had suckered herself to the soft white underbelly of her soul, slowly leeching the life force from her.

"I HATE YOU!" she screamed at her. "I'VE ALWAYS HATED YOU!"

Regina prattled on about how she had only given birth to her because it was the right and necessary thing. She spoke of her daughter like a white grub she'd squeezed from her loins and nourished on royal jelly so that she might take her rightful place in the hive.

"YOU DON'T EVEN CARE THAT I FUCKING DESPISE YOU!" Javy cried out.

At that moment, she realized there was a painting on the wall behind Regina's chair. In it, a man of gleaming onyx sat on a throne, hundreds of naked human beings wriggling at his feet like plump maggots. He was the Messenger, Javy knew, and he and only he understood the greater plan for mankind. He watched her with glistening spider eyes, grinning at her, because he knew all and she knew nothing.

Javy strode toward Regina.

She was going to kill her, she was going to vanquish her evil for once and all. She would crush her with the hydraulic-driven arms of the suit. She would mash her to paste and, in doing so, would feel free for the first time in her life.

But…Regina was changing. She was mutating into some horrendous benthic life-form. Her flesh had gone gray and was made of huge overlapping scales. It was oily and shiny like wet sealskin. Her limbs were weirdly contoured with bony V-shaped ridges that pushed up from under her skin. Her eyes were huge and glassy like those of a fish. When she reached out a hand to her daughter, the fingers were long and clawed, a fine webbing between each finger.

Javy screamed because this was the *real* Regina. It was insane and impossible and couldn't possibly be, but it was: here was the true Regina that had been hiding under her mother's skin. Her head narrowed like that of a wolffish, her lips huge and blubbery. A spiny ridge ran from her forehead and over the crown of her head. Gill slits fluttered at her neck.

"I didn't want you. I did not want *their* seed growing in me...but it was predestined that I bring you to term. That I keep you and feed you, nurture you like a fingerling in a hatchery until the time came when I could release you into the silent depths," Regina told her. "Oh, but I *sinned*. I turned against them. I disobeyed the teachings of the elder ones. I kept you from the water. I would not listen when they called for you. I coveted you because you were *mine* and I would never let them have you! Never let them take you down into the deeps. I would not have you swimming down in the weeds and rotting shipwrecks...you would never know the crystalline cities at the bottom of the sea."

"Stop it!" Javy shrieked. *"I won't hear anymore! You disgust me! Everything about you disgusts me!"*

Regina had risen now, a mutant, ichthyic horror that had evolved to live in the darkest depths of the oceans. "I tried to keep them from you. I *tried!* But you wouldn't keep away from the water. You were drawn to it. Deep inside you, you wanted to return to them, to dive amongst the ancient reefs and offer yourself at the sunken Temple of Dagon—"

But Javy would hear no more.

She jetted from the chamber and through the tunnel and she was back in the enclosing forest of tube worms, moving through them like a mouse through a field of wheat.

"You cannot escape your destiny," Regina whispered in her head. *"I warned you...I always tried to warn you. But now you are here. You went down the rabbit hole, Alice, and now you'll never be free. The city will rise and you'll rise with it..."*

Regina was coming after her. No longer speaking, she pushed through the worm stalks, her mouth opening and closing, her arms tentacles, bloodlessly white and set with huge pulsating suckers. They reached out for her daughter. They would coil around her and crush the life from her in this secret jungle of tube worms.

(Alice)

She was coming fast now, snapping right through the wavering tube worms. Knocking them aside, felling them like trees, screeching her displeasure in Javy's head with a white-hot explosion of noise like a thousand squealing rats.

(Alice)

Inside her helmet, Javy's head shook from side to side. That awful noise. God, that awful noise. It put her guts in her throat, made her shake even as sweat rolled down her face. Her entire body seemed to be throbbing with pure terror.

(Alice don't you dare turn away from me)

Javy realized she had stopped now and the tube worms had given way to a forest of seaweed and green kelp. Strands and ropes of it knotted up the suit, slowing her forward progress. She was stuck in the weeds like a fly in the web of a house spider. Regina's white tentacles were seeking her out, sliding through the weeds like eels, their suckers puckering now like pink, hungry mouths.

(ALICE DON'T YOU DARE TURN FROM ME)

Javy knew that the city was powering the apparition that stalked her. But it couldn't do a damn thing without her mind, without her twisted, disturbing memories and the raw psionic force of her imagination. Only she could break the connection between them. Only she could unplug her mind from the socket of the city and exorcize Regina.

(ALICE ALICE ALICE ALICE)

Regina squealing in her head, Javy fought from the weeds and snaking reeds, tearing through them just as Regina's coiling tentacles were mere feet away, her fish-mouth opening to reveal a set of fine needle-like teeth. Her eyes were huge and dead like those of a barracuda, her hair swimming around her narrowed skull like the snakes of Medusa.

Javy escaped and exited the city after a mad journey down one tunnel after another, but even then, she knew she had not escaped at all.

21
TEN MINUTES TO MIDNIGHT

Sitting in his cabin, Orr realized with a biting, raw misery that they had made a terrible mistake coming here, going through with all this. Not himself or the team below or the mechanics, as it were, of the op, but the NSF and ONI, all the big boys up top, the puppet-masters and power-players. They had seriously underestimated what was going on in Antarctica and particularly at Kharkov Station and the lake below. They were toying with something that was best left alone. Certain boxes were meant to be kept shut and certain scabs should not have been picked at.

Don't fool yourself, he told himself. *They knew. They knew exactly what kind of mess this was. You and the rest of the Vordog team were lambs they led carefully to slaughter. Don't pretend otherwise, because you know it's true.*

"Too late," he said to himself in the darkness. "It's all too late now."

And maybe, somehow, he had known this the very moment he arrived at Kharkov with the DSSD engineering team and got a feel for the station, stepped into the drill tower and looked down into the hole they were boring into the ice. Surely he should have known it when he got a good look at the faces of the maintenance crew and the drill team… pale and pinched, rarely smiling, eyes like non-reflective glass. *Haunted.* Every one of them haunted. And if he hadn't known it then, he should have known it when his own headaches started and those godawful dreams began plaguing him.

Yes, he should have known.

Sitting there, his head throbbing like a bad tooth filled with infection, he tried to think, tried to put it in perspective in a larger sense as had always been his way. But there was nothing. Just that curious blankness and lethargy he'd brought with him out of the dreams. He'd been awake maybe ten minutes and the dreams were fading, but their hold on him was strong, organically-rooted. He could remember tossing and turning, haunted and terrified, waking cold and shaking and sweaty, a scream locked in his throat.

And he could remember…remember…

The city…those things hovering above the city…and he was one of them…

He felt like he was going mad. But deeper down, he knew it was something else entirely. Something was reaching out for him, wanting to convert him and remake him in its own hideous image.

Swallowing the dryness in his throat, he turned on the light, trying to control his breathing, trying to remember that he was an officer of the United States Navy and he had to continue mission regardless of how he felt.

He squatted before the little safe in the closet. He keyed in the combination and took out the sealed orders he had been given. Sitting at his desk, he broke the seal on them and took out a folder in a red plastic binder marked NAVCOM/TOP SECRET, and beneath that, EYES ONLY.

His palms began to sweat. His fingers trembled. He expected terrible things and he was not disappointed. The first fifteen pages were pretty much what he expected—the Lake Vordog mission profile. A series of potentialities that were to be enacted for various situations. And then, on the final page, the desperate eleventh-hour solution should all else fail.

Oh Jesus.

He was shocked, but not surprised. Deep down, he had expected something like this, something catastrophic. Angry, he closed the folder and put it back in the safe. He was supposed to burn it after reading, but he didn't bother.

He memorized what it said.

He was now the caretaker of a terrible secret.

22
POLLYANNA IS DEAD

After they were back from the city and duly sorted out, Bell began to ask questions because he needed answers. For nearly two hours, Javonivic and Hubbs had been out of radio contact. He kept asking Javy about it, but he did not receive the answers he wanted. Something had changed in her and he could not quite identify what it was, only that he did not like it. She was always so outgoing, so positive, so motivated, so very dedicated to the mission at hand and the well-being of the team itself. She was a light to see by and a force of nature to be reckoned with.

Or she had been.

Now, as she sat across from him in the galley, she was withdrawn, pale, barely even there. She did not smile. She did not emote. Something had been taken from her, leaving a gaping, bottomless void inside her.

"I need to know what happened in there," he told her, not phrasing it like an order, but a simple friendly request.

She laughed. It startled him. Her face did not laugh, nor did her eyes. Only her mouth and it had a dry, awful sound to it like a puppet.

"Javy, talk to me."

She swallowed a couple of times. "We went into the city. We lost communications. I could hear you trying to contact me, but I couldn't reply. Hubbs and I got separated, I guess. We found our way out."

Bell sighed. It was like trying to hold a conversation with a wax dummy. He might as well have dropped a dime into her. He'd already spoken with Hubbs at some length, and what he'd gotten from him hadn't made much sense. Madness about monsters and living machines. Strictly subjective stuff. He was counting on Javy to give him a slightly more balanced, objective view of things.

"I want to know what happened in there," he told her. "I want your assessment of the situation. I'm not just asking you for it now, I'm ordering you to tell me."

She nodded. "Okay, sir. I'll give you my assessment—blow that fucking place up."

"Which is pretty much what Hubbs told me."

"And he's right. The city is a machine. It generates fear and anxiety. It knows what scares you, what disturbs you, and it plucks it from your mind and uses it against you to break you down. To take away your will. To enslave you. Make you part of it. It has to be destroyed. That's my assessment."

Bell thought it over. He watched her carefully. It was obvious that there was more to tell, but she held back. Whatever it was, it pained her deeply and he wondered what sort of personal trauma of hers it had externalized. It had pretty much done the same thing to Murphy.

And the scariest part was that he believed what she said.

"Hubbs told me that every time we go in there, that much less of us comes out." She shrugged. "I thought he was crazy. But you know what, Chief? He's not. He really pegged it this time, regardless of how nuts it sounds."

He cleared his throat. "You want me to tell Orr this? Because, you know what? He's going to ask."

"Yes. Tell him."

"I can pretty much tell you what his reaction will be."

The ice she had encased herself in began to crack and he could feel her fuming inside, ready to burst. "Honestly, Chief, I don't give a damn what his reaction is. The Navy put us in a terrible position here. If we don't destroy that city, it'll destroy us." She held up a hand when he opened his mouth. "It's already sunk its teeth into us. It's already invaded our dreams.

It's devouring us bit by bit and it'll never stop until we're nothing but bones. We need to destroy it, then get the hell out of here. It'll never let us leave if we don't destroy it."

By that point, Bell's body had gone stiff. As a military man, his posture was never completely relaxed, always somewhat rigid. But right then, he was stiff as a plank. If he tightened up much more, his spine would crack.

"Javy," he said, "we can leave anytime we want. That's always an option. We can take the submersible up to the LSB. Orr will have our asses for lunch if we scrub the mission, but we can do it."

She shook her head. "You're wrong, sir. We can't leave—the city won't let us. If we try to, the submersible will be gone or it will be sabotaged. If we get into it, it'll be crushed like a can."

"And who would sabotage it? The bogies?"

"No. *We* would. One of us might have already crippled it beyond repair. We wouldn't even remember doing it."

Which, again, was pretty much what Hubbs had said. That the city could rewrite their minds, making them forget things that had happened and implant false memories. Whatever served its end. It was absolutely insane, yet, despite what his rational mind told him, he could not disregard any of it.

The big problem, of course, was proof. In that, there was none. Both Javy and Hubbs made some fantastic, distressing claims, but there was no verification of any of it. The Exosuits kept a video log of everything, but the feed and backup of it was completely blanked out from the time they entered the city to the time they came back out. Nothing but static.

And what did that say?

That some outside agency had blacked it out? Bell didn't for a minute doubt that was impossible. What he was having trouble with was their sketchy—very sketchy—version of events. If what Hubbs was saying was even partially true, then their memories of events could have been completely distorted.

Like yours aren't.

He thought about telling her a few things, one of which was what Murph said happened with the attacking faces…but, no, he wasn't going to do that. This particular blaze was burning just fine without him feeding it.

"You really believe all this?" he asked her, because he had to.

She stared at him a long time. Her eyes were wet with fear. "Yes, and I think, deep down, you do, too. We've all been contaminated by the city. There's something wrong with all of us now. Hubbs is seeing things and I'm not sure they're hallucinations. I heard what Murph was saying over the radio, that he was attacked by something."

"And you?"

She chewed at her lower lip. "I'm being tormented by the worst thing I can imagine—my mother. She's been dead for years. But down here, she's not dead enough." Javy sipped from her water bottle. "How about you, Chief? What's that damn city doing to you?"

But that was something he dared not admit to anyone.

23
MEMORY LANE

Later, Bell got on the comm and had a chat with Orr, for all the good it did him. He told him everything. What was true to the best of his knowledge, what might be true, and those things he could not substantiate (namely, the claims of Murph, Hubbs, and Javy). He laid it all out as linear and systematically as possible, the way he would have in any report to his superiors.

"And you want to scrub it on the basis of this?" Orr asked him. "Hallucinations? Delusions? Mental aberrations? C'mon, Chief. I'll be the first one to admit there's something bad about that city…there's a power to it, but if we scrub because of this…*shit,* you know what's going to happen. You've got a great record. Do you really want this going into your file?"

"I want to keep my people safe, sir."

Orr was silent for a few moments, then he said, "They'll toss you out of the DSU, Chief. You and your divers. Your career is over and so is theirs. That's all I'm saying. I put this over the network and you're done. They will be no going back."

It was suicide and Bell knew it. But Javy, Hubbs, and Murph meant the world to him. Yet, he knew he had to proceed carefully now. It wasn't just the brass of the DSU he had to worry about, but the spooks of ONI and the heavy thinkers of the ONR all the way up to the Vice Admiral of CENTCOM and the political dynamos and shadow players behind the

NSF. There were a lot of hands in on this one and they were powerful hands that could crush careers and reputations in their bare fists. And Orr was warning him that he was about to tread in shark-infested waters.

He's worried about us, but he's also worried about himself, Bell thought. *The lot of us are here by his recommendation. If we scrub or fail, he'll never get the mud off his face.*

But was that it? Was that really it? Orr always put his people's safety first. He was solid and dependable. Bell felt guilty even thinking that his superior was playing politics. But there was something there. Even over the comm, he could sense it: something unsaid. An undercurrent of danger.

What is he saying without actually saying it?

Orr sighed. "Chief, you know I have your back. Tell me what you want me to do...just please consider it very carefully. The DSU can't afford to lose you and your people."

"I'm conflicted, sir."

"You want my advice? Continue mission for a few more days. If, at that time, you're still in this frame of mind, then we pull the plug."

"Okay, sir. Let's proceed with that."

Bell had the most terrible feeling that he was letting his divers down, but what Orr was telegraphing him was that there was a lot more at stake here than careers, unless he was reading it completely wrong. But he'd been living by his instinct for so long by that point, that he didn't think so.

"Tell me something," Orr said. "You've been in the city. Have you seen anything unusual?"

Before he could say anything problematic, he quickly said, "Not a thing."

"Well, let's play it out for a few days," Orr told him. "In the meantime, find that damn anomaly source, Chief."

"Yes, sir."

Orr signed off and Bell sat there, tense, worried, his skin crawling.

Have you seen anything unusual?

That was the problem: Bell could have answered both yes and no. His memories were scrambled. His guts told him that he hadn't seen a thing, but his memory told him that he had. That was the scary part.

What had Hubbs told him? *That city can erase memories, Chief, and write new ones. What you remember might not be the truth. You might be suppressing things that are too awful to remember. Then again, maybe I'm losing my mind.*

And that was it, wasn't it? That was the fear that nipped away at Bell. He'd had a strange, inexplicable paranoia since he was a teenager that his memories were suspect. It made no sense, yet the fear of it was pervasive. A secret terror he'd never admitted to no one.

The root of it was his Uncle Bernie.

He'd been a very sweet, kind, lovable man who owned a butcher shop in Passaic, New Jersey. One day, distracted as he often was, he stepped out into traffic and was struck by a speeding minivan. He was thrown head-first to the curb. It took thirty-three stitches to close his scalp. He was in a coma for six days. When he came out of it, he didn't recognize anyone. He didn't have amnesia per se—he remembered his job, his name, his history—but his family and friends were strangers to him. He kept calling out for his nonexistent wife (Rhonda), his nonexistent children (Bobby and Clara), and his equally nonexistent brother (Joseph).

He could not be talked out of this delusion and became convinced that a conspiracy of some sort was in place. Then, as therapy continued and the weeks passed, it all faded. It was temporary, but frightening. To Bell, the scariest part was how certain Uncle Bernie was of his imaginary family's existence. He even had detailed memories, backstories, and histories for each of them.

Though his mom told him crazy things like that happened with head trauma, inside, Bell had trouble accepting it. It had made him uneasy for a long time. Even into adulthood, there had been a nagging fear as to the nature—and reliability—of memory.

And what had stirred all of this back up was the city and what he had seen there. *Or not seen.* Like all the divers, he had written up a detailed account of his excursions into the ruins. And, as of yesterday, he had found a terrible discrepancy. What he had written of his second jaunt into the city with Murphy was not what he remembered at all. It was a dry essay of endless tunnels and exploration, but not much else.

His memory was quite different.

He remembered the darkness of the passages, the tiny creatures swimming around them, the whirling globs of sediment in their lights. And...*Javy*. He remembered her being with him, which was patently untrue because Murphy had been his dive partner.

Yet, the memory was strong.

Javy and he entered a chamber that was vaguely ovoid in shape. There was nothing very exceptional about it; it looked very much like many of them did: the marine growths, the weeds, the mats of green algae etc. Yet, upon entering it, he had felt a slowly-building fear take hold of him that gradually escalated to full-blown terror when he saw what was hanging on the walls. Javy had found it and immediately drew his attention to it. When Bell got his lights over there, he saw what made her eyes go wide beneath the acrylic bubble of her face shield: two bodies hanging from the wall, their limbs moving in the current with a slow, feathering motion. They were both male and both naked, bloated white things like human slugs, their flesh torn by hungry crustaceans and nibbled by fish, streamers of it floating around them like strands of confetti. Neither had eyes and both had the huge, rubbery mouths of sucker fish.

"It's Murphy and Hubbs," Javy had said. "Dear God, it's Murphy and Hubbs."

Bell did not try to convince her otherwise, because there was no mistaking it. But it couldn't be. It just couldn't be. They were back at the Neptune. And—according to Bell's report written in his own hand—Javy wasn't with him at all.

"The bogies," Javy said in small, wounded voice.

"What do you mean?"

"The bogies got them."

"These are fakes, Javy. They have to be."

They looked unpleasantly real, but if they weren't fakes, then who was back at the Neptune?

As Bell sat there, remembering it all, he felt more disturbed than ever. Surely, he was confusing what really happened with a dream. It had to be. He knew he went to the city each time with Murphy. He'd never gone with Javy. Hubbs was her dive partner. His report verified that. But why was his recall of the episode with Javy so damn strong?

Maybe he should have told Orr about it, but he hadn't dared. There was an answer to this. Maybe the bogies had implanted it in his head to toy with him. Maybe what Hubbs had said was true. Regardless, his old paranoia concentrating the veracity of memory was back in full force and he felt like he was lost in the maze of his own mind, unable to differentiate between reality and fantasy, real memory and that which might have been implanted.

All of which was unacceptable.

He was in charge down here and people were counting on him. He couldn't weaken. He couldn't lose his nerve. He knew, *knew* he'd gone in the city with Murphy. Games were being played and he had to fight against them.

Two more days.

Just two more days.

That's what Orr said. He only wished he believed him.

24

SEA MONSTER

Many hours later, in the midst of a thin and tortured sleep, Javonivic woke to the smell of rotting flesh. It was sickening, yes, but also absolutely impossible. This was the stink of something dead for many weeks—green and gaseous—and it simply couldn't be.

She sat up, but it did not fade. She was reminded of the time as a child when they'd returned from two weeks visiting her aunt in St. Michael only to discover that the refrigerator had puked out in their absence. The house had smelled like rotting fish, courtesy of the six pounds of bluefish tuna steaks in the freezer that had gone most decidedly bad. Regina had practically gone out of her mind.

But smelling it here in the habitat, in her cabin…it made no sense. She turned on the light, but could find nothing to explain the smell. As she prepared to go track down the source, she had the most horrible of realizations—the smell was coming from her.

The stink was wafting from her skin in hot, nauseating waves. It couldn't be. But as she sniffed first her hoodie, then her arms, there was no doubt of it. The rot was coming from *inside* of her as if she was filled with decomposing fish.

Suddenly, she was slick with sweat, shaking and feverish. Even her breath stank like a beach at low tide. It was gagging. As she tried to make it to the door, her head spun with vertigo and she went down to her knees. She vomited a clear, greenish bile onto the floor. And there was no doubting what she saw in it—fish scales and tiny bones.

She let out a scream and fell back against her bunk, wiping her mouth with her arm.

And then, as if all that physical horror was a prelude, it began. There was a skittering feeling inside her head like her skull was filled with tiny gray mice. She could feel them digging inside her brain, creating white jolts of pain that made her cry out. Colors flashed before her eyes. It felt like her entire body was throbbing.

What is this? What the hell is this?

But then she knew as she heard that crackling noise in her head once again, followed by the scraping/scratching sound. Her eyes peeled open. There were voices in her mind, garbled voices all shrieking simultaneously. Their volume amplified until she pressed her hands to ears and screamed. She fell over, crawling on her belly, inching forward. It was Regina. Her voice was calling out of the black depths and she was forcing herself into Javy's head, trying to find the proper wavelength and make contact.

No, no, no! Go away, you fucking witch!

Javy got through the door, managing to climb uneasily to her feet, stumbling down the short corridor, bouncing off the bulkheads. All the while, Regina's voice cut through the static in her head, rising to a shrill, feverish pitch. Seconds later, she made her way into the control center. And they were all there—Bell, Hubbs, and Murphy. Alarms were ringing off. The motion detectors outside the habitat had been triggered. The sonar alarm was whining.

"What is it?" she asked, damp with sweat and shivering with fright. "What in the hell is it?"

"Something's out there," Murphy said, studying the sonar screen. "Something big."

On the screen, the habitat was a large red triangle at the center. At the outer edge was a red circle, the seabed echo as read by the sensor as it rotated. And hovering about the habitat was a quickly darting, red blob, which was their visitor.

Bell was in the galley, staring out of one of the bubble viewports, trying to get a look at what was out there. Hubbs was with him. Both looked pale and tense.

"Some kind of creature," Bell said. "I caught only a glimpse of it."

Hubbs nodded slowly. "I saw something white like a tentacle, but just for a second. It looked like that thing that Orr showed us, the image from Gundry's cryobot five years back."

Javy looked out the ports, but saw nothing in the outer lights, just the lake out there—cold, dark, and forbidding. That voice was still trying to get into her head, but at least that awful fishy odor was gone. There were reasons for it, she knew, but she honestly didn't want to know what they were.

She crossed over to the hatch that led into the rec room. There were more viewports there. As she approached them, the voice rang out in her head, each reverberation sinking into her brain like an icepick.

(Alice Alice Alice)

Javy made her way to one of the viewports, bracing her hands against the bulkhead so she didn't go right over.

In the light of the exterior halogens, she caught sight of a blurry figure whose image gradually sharpened until she saw that it was Regina—as perfectly hideous and grotesque as she had been in the city: an undulant, boneless horror like a human eel. Her spreading, spiny fins were slightly luminous, red-tipped gills quivering at her throat, her mouth like that of a channel catfish with twisting, whip-like barbels growing from her swollen lips.

"No, no, no," Javy muttered, suppressing the scream that begged to be voided, her muscles gone lax, her body shuddering. She could barely stay on her feet.

Regina watched her with the huge, lidless eyes of an abyssal fish, her tentacle arms coiling obscenely, the suckers on their undersides anxious to rip the flesh from her bones.

(ALICE DO NOT TURN AWAY FROM ME)

Now Javy did scream as she bicycled backwards and crashed to the floor. She clutched her head in her hands as Regina shrieked at her. Her mind was like a radio locked on a single station and the volume was being turned louder and louder and louder until it seemed like her skull would crack open.

(ALICE LOOK AT ME ALICE)

And then Bell was there, pulling her to her feet. He cast a look out the viewport and it was obvious he saw something, at least a quick glimpse of it, then he helped Javy back to the the control center.

"Javy," he said. "Javy…c'mon, talk to me…"

But she found that she was incapable. Her thoughts were jumbled, her mind echoing with that awful, strident voice, and her mouth just couldn't seem to form words. Her eyes were fixed on dead space, seeing something no one else could.

"She looks like she's in shock," Murphy said.

Her mouth opened and closed. Her face was twisted in a smirk. Finally, she said, *"Mama…mama's coming…"*

At that moment, something hit the Neptune. And whatever it was, it must have had the raw, bull strength of a battering whale to make the entire structure shake. Bell was thrown against the bulkhead. Hubbs crashed into Murphy. Javy's head whipped back and forth, her body jerking with muscular spasms.

Alarms were ringing out, echoing through Main Lock. Computer screens flickered. Lights flashed. And then it was hit again. Everyone was dumped to the floor. The lights flickered and the habitat was thrown into the seamless blackness of the bottom of the lake. A pressure relief valve down the corridor blew, spraying jets of water. Rivets popped in the ceiling, one of them bouncing around like a ricocheted bullet.

"It's attacking us!" Murphy called out. *"It's goddamn well attacking us!"*

The emergency lights came on weakly like guttering candles. Javy crawled across the floor, saying things under her breath that no one else could hear in the cacophony and which she could not even understand herself.

(ALICE ALICE NOW IS THE TIME NOW I COME FOR YOU YOU CANNOT ESCAPE YOUR DESTINY)

"Fuck you!" Javy screamed. *"Leave us alone, you miserable fucking witch! You cunt! You fucking bitch go away go away! GO THE FUCK AWAY!"*

Hubbs pulled himself to his feet, using the console to steady himself, backing as far away from Javy as he could get. "It's her! It's her!" he cried. *"She called it! She summoned it out of the city!"*

The habitat was hit again and more rivets went shooting in every which direction. Through one of the ports, she saw a huge white tentacle that had to be as big around as a telephone pole slap against the window, its suckers and their attendant hooks tearing at the glass. The Neptune groaned and creaked. It seemed like it might crush like an aluminum can in a fist... then, the attack stopped.

Everything was quiet save for alarms which died out one after the other.

Water dripped.

Steam hissed.

There was nothing on the sonar screen.

All the exterior lights came back on as well as the ones inside. Everyone slowly, carefully, got to their feet. Their faces were sweaty, eyes bulging, mouths trembling.

"What in the hell was that?" Bell finally managed to say.

Hubbs chuckled with a derisive sound. "Ask Javy. She knows. Oh, she knows very well."

But that was impossible: she had gone out cold.

25
BIG BROTHER

Bell, of course, was more adamant than ever about scrubbing the op. He wanted his people out of the Neptune and up to Kharkov Station. It seemed a perfectly reasonable idea, but Orr was hesitant. He had reasons to be. And all of them were locked up in the operational orders in his safe. He wanted to tell Bell what the contingency plan was, but, of course, that would have been a violation of protocol.

And let's face it, he thought then. *Communications between the LSB and the Neptune are probably being monitored.*

If the ONI found out that he was scrubbing the mission without their permission, they just might decide to execute the contingency plans from their end. Something which was certainly possible. No doubt they'd already run a detailed threat analysis and had a strategy in place in case Orr (or anyone else) compromised the mission.

You're swimming in very murky seas. Don't forget that. And the people behind this are extremely ruthless.

When you were in a first-class pig fuck like this, Orr knew, trust was sometimes an endangered species or it was already extinct. There was no way to know if everything that was going on in the LSB and the Neptune was constantly monitored. It sounded paranoid, but when you dealt with the sort of groups that were behind the Lake Vordog mission, paranoia was not a weakness, but an asset. It was quite possible that there were plants in the Kharkov Station crew or in the drill tower crew. Hell, Anderson, for all he knew, might be one of them.

The attack on the habitat had not been a blind act of rage, though for those below it had seemed that way. The purpose of it was to disable the submersible that would bring the dive team up to the LSB. Something, of course, which had been accomplished. The submersible was not only disabled…it was gone. The creature had stripped it free of its moorings and taken it away. It probably lay crushed in some deep abyss.

There were still the escape pods. And the hardsuits. Both of which could get the team to the LSB safely. But if that happened, would the dread contingency plan be set into motion?

Orr had considered taking the LSB's submersible down to pick up the team…but if they showed up at Kharkov, would someone in the station alert command of the breach of operation?

Christ, but they were in a spot.

Orr sat there, wanting a drink very badly. The dive team was in incredible danger down there. But they might be in worse danger if they dared return to the surface.

He thought of what was in the safe and it made him feel not only hopeless, but doomed.

26
AFTERMATH

The air inside the hardsuit tasted metallic.

Gritty and dry, like sucking wind through a metal pipe. That's what occurred to Bell as the hydraulic winch lowered both he and Murphy through the moon pool and down into the lake itself. Below the level of the Neptune habitat itself, the clamps released them and they sank slowly down to the baseplate which supported the entire structure above.

"Just take it real easy," Javonivic said over the comm.

"We're fine, Javy," Murphy said. "I think our beastie is long gone."

"Yes, of course. But take it slow."

This was the point, Bell knew, where Murph and Javy usually started joking with each other, but there was no good cheer or humor in the air today. Everyone was wound tight. They were scared and they had good reason to be.

"Hubbs, just make sure you don't take your eyes off sonar," Murphy said.

"I'm glued to it."

The Exosuits, of course, had their own sonar, but Bell wanted as many eyes on them as possible. He had always felt uneasy in the lake, but that fear was always vague and unformed, but now it had taken on shape. It was physical and dangerous. In his many years as a diver, he'd encountered everything from deadly box jellyfish to voracious squid to highly-aggressive bull sharks, but none of them disturbed him like the creature that had attacked the habitat. It was in a league of its own.

The real problem was Lake Vordog itself and that damn city. You couldn't always believe what you saw.

Murphy and he stood on the baseplate, looking around.

Maybe they both knew they weren't going to find anything, but Orr up in the LSB told them to look, see if they could find any trace of the submersible. It was a highly-expensive piece of technology to lose. It was pointless, though, Bell figured, what had destroyed it no doubt did a thorough job of it. It wasn't even sending a homing beacon.

Sonar showed squat. Not so much as a bubble. The high-magnification lenses of the suit's pan-and-tilt video systems revealed nothing. And, standing there, both of them doing a 360 with video and their own eyes, there was still nothing. Nothing at all. Just the baseplate beneath them, the Neptune above. The SDVs moored to the legs.

Bell kept looking.

Above him, the Neptune resembled a flying saucer sitting on its four, massive legs. The legs were lit by security lights as was the outside of the habitat itself. It was circular, flattened like a disk, a light every four feet right around its edge.

"Looks pretty tame out there," Javonivic said.

"Not a thing," Bell said.

Beyond the lights, the lake was murky with an almost greenish tint to it, lots of drifting sediment. It looked pretty peaceful.

"Well, you boys gonna stand there or what?" she wanted to know.

"You hear that, Chief?" Murphy said over the intercom. "First she don't want us to leave, now she wants to get rid of us."

"We're going for a walk," Bell told her.

"That's my boys."

She was holding up well. Last night, the attack had been pretty traumatic on all of them, but particularly on her. Hubbs was still insisting that she had called the creature, that the city had taken her deep-set fear of her mother and gave it physical form. The very idea was way out there... yet, nobody really doubted it completely. Particularly, Javy herself. She felt responsible and nothing Bell said could seem to talk her out of it.

We've all seen and felt things, he thought as he moved around the baseplate with Murphy. *Scary, unpleasant things…but nothing's been as deadly or corporeal as the creature. Why is that? Why was Javy's fear so much more devastating?*

Then again, he realized, maybe she had nothing to do with it. Maybe the creature was simply a nightmare denizen of the lake, perhaps attracted by the habitat lights the way giant squid were sometimes drawn to deep-sea drilling platforms. Maybe. Possibly. But whatever it was, it attacked with fury, seemingly targeting the submersible.

No, there's nothing random about this.

And more the reason Orr should have been sending the other submersible down for the team. But he wasn't. And there was a reason for that, Bell just wished he knew what it was.

The bottom line was that they were all feeling the strain. And it wasn't going to get any better. Orr seemed determined that they tough it out and locate the anomaly. Something which Bell thought was now incalculably dangerous.

"Any action on the screen?" he said over the comm.

"Nothing. Very quiet," Hubbs told him.

He was still his old dour self. Ever since his first trip to the city, he'd been a little off. And with each succeeding voyage he'd gotten a little more so. He wouldn't say what was really bothering him; he just dropped his daily quota of spooky, mystical remarks. Things which made no sense or maybe they made all the sense in the world (depending on your viewpoint). But in his eyes, there was always that funny look like maybe he knew lots of things, weird and scary things, that he could tell you all about if he chose to. Only he didn't choose to.

Your team is fragmenting and you know it. The question is: what are you going to do about it?

Staying in visual range, Bell and Murphy scouted around on the baseplate with brief thrusts of their suit jets, moving in ever-widening concentric circles.

"Pretty dull down here," Murphy said.

Bell wasn't sure. It looked dead and harmless, yes…but was it?

He just wasn't sure.

He'd seen too much now to trust his eyes.

What you saw in Lake Vordog was not necessarily what was really there. They all still suffered from the headaches that came and went with no reason; they were all having the nightmares; and everyone was plagued by that uncanny feeling of being watched or studied, an unsettling sense that there was someone or something right behind them at times…so close that if they turned really quick, they'd be staring it dead in the face. And how much of the latter was imagination and paranoia, it was hard to say.

But tangible, terrible things had happened, of course.

Besides the attack on the habitat, Javonivic claimed to have seen shadowy forms swimming past the viewport in Main Lock and Murphy claimed that there had been something huge, white, and fleshy with about a dozen eyes staring up at him from the moon pool. And Javonivic had woken at like three in the morning a few days ago, claiming something had touched her. Something slimy and cold. Just a nightmare? Well, that didn't explain the pool of water next to her bed or that inexplicable, dank smell like rotting weeds that hung in the air.

While Murphy scouted around the legs, Bell pressed the vertical thruster footpads and went up. He looked around the bottom of the habitat. There were no signs of damage, other than a few deeply-embedded scratches that had not been there before. The shell was designed to take a great deal of abuse. So either whatever it was hadn't been strong enough to cause any trouble or it hadn't been trying to.

I vote for the latter, he thought as Murphy joined him and they made a trip around the habitat itself. *If it was strong enough to shake the Neptune, it could have done a lot more. It was a scare tactic. But to what end? Just to take the submersible out of the picture? Or was there more to it?*

The point being, they could still reach the surface, but the apparent destruction of the submersible was like a symbolic gesture to show them that they weren't going anywhere.

They spent another hour out there making their rounds. Whatever had been at the habitat last night, shaking it out of mere curiosity or because it was directed to, it left no further evidence behind.

Finally, Javy came over the headset: "Cash it in, Chief. Nothing out there, I guess."

"Will do," he said.

As they made their way back to the moon pool, Bell was relieved. He didn't like the idea that there was only the shell of his hardsuit in-between whatever was out there and himself. Maybe they hadn't seen it, but it was there.

God yes, like a hungry tiger circling in the dark jungle, it was most certainly there.

27

DOOMSDAY

Every time they entered the city, Bell wondered if it would be his last.

As monstrous and alien as it was, it was also an absolute maze. A honeycombed labyrinth of horizontal tunnels and vertical channels, octagonal rooms and sphere-shaped compartments, oval cells and gigantic tubular amphitheaters that seemed to have no beginning and no end. Rooms terminated into other rooms. Tunnels split into dozens of spiraling burrows. Massive upright cylindrical chambers hundreds and hundreds of feet in diameter were set with thousands of cavities and very often crowded with winding helix-shaped structures or vast networks of hollow piping that seemed to serve no purpose whatsoever.

It was insane and claustrophobic, at least to the human mind. In the many days that they had been exploring it and mapping it out—at least their little corner of it-Bell had realized that there was a symmetry to it. Unearthly perhaps, but it was there. And once he had shut down that awful sense of déjà vu and the superstitious terror that threaded through him, he was able to see this. It made sense to those who built it. It was wholly utilitarian to the minds that conceived of it. No earthly mind, of course, would ever make sense of it or hope to grasp the mathematical concepts it was based upon. The angles were all wrong, the uniformity positively perverse.

But it was there. If your mind could only grasp it.

Thirty minutes into it, the uneasiness and anxiety began to fade and he was able to see the job ahead of them and the path they must take. Even if he himself could not remember the way in or out, his Exosuit did. Its onboard computers carefully guided him via sonar.

Today was the day.

Murphy and he were both lugging the lockboxes of RDX Comtac explosives. If they found the source of the magnetic anomaly—and that seemed a pretty sure thing given that Javonivic and Hubbs had been very close to it two days before—they would activate the explosives and get out.

And this would be their last trip.

They moved down a rectangular passage that was big enough to drive a tractor trailer through. It was thick with marine growths and waving sea grass. Sediment drifted in their lights.

"ETA about fifteen minutes," Murphy said over the suit intercom. "Shouldn't be far after that."

Fifteen minutes would bring them to the hexagonal chamber Javonivic and Hubbs had mapped out. The anomaly couldn't be much further on.

"Shouldn't be."

"Let's get drunk for a week after this, Chief."

"I'm with you on that."

"Keep your eyes open," Javonivic said over the radio.

"Will do," Murphy told her. "You hear a sound, it's just my knees knocking together."

Of course, Javonivic wasn't there with them, but she was seeing what they were seeing just as Orr was up in the LSB. Their first few trips into the city, they had gone in blind. No audio, no video. They assumed it was the structure itself or perhaps the density of the water and its unusual atmospheric pressure caused by the glacier above pressing down upon the lake. But it was none of these things. Simply a defective fiber-optic line in the umbilical leading from the Neptune to the LSB on the surface. Orr and his techie had fixed it and now they were no longer alone...even in this place which was lonely as lonely got.

The ADS hardsuits transmitted their data to the Neptune which transmitted it up to the LSB. It was part of a microwave telemetry system called the WWN, the Wireless Wave Network. Through it, they had instantaneous audio, video, and data transmission back and forth.

"And here I thought that rapping was the beat of your heart for me," Javonivic said.

Murphy laughed. "Why you always coming on to me when I can't touch you, Javy?"

"It's part of my mystique."

"Tease."

"Mostly."

Orr came over the radio as Bell knew he would. "All right, all right, people. Let's keep this professional, all right? ONR, ONI, and NSF are going to be listening to this stuff and they're not gonna be much interested in your unrequited love for one another."

"Roger that," Bell said.

Murphy grunted. "They're jealous, Javy, that's all."

"Don't I know it."

The fiber-optic line was only part of the communication problem, Bell knew. It still didn't explain how they were transmitting and receiving just fine now, but hadn't been able to at all on their first excursions into the city. Everyone was aware of that, but like many things concerning the city, they preferred not to talk about it.

They pushed on, moving through honeycombed rooms and arched passageways. They saw lots of marine growths and suspended fields of silt, a few stray jellyfish or crabs, but not much else. They guided the suits finally down a triangular-shaped conduit that seemed to go on forever.

"This is it," Murphy said.

It took them nearly ten minutes to navigate its length. At the end, there was a stygian murkiness that their lights would barely penetrate. Then they punched through it and it was just another blizzard of algae.

"We reached your chamber, Javy," Bell said.

Her transmission broke up momentarily with static, but they caught the very end of it. "...happened to us. Watch it now."

This was as far as any of the divers had gotten. Sonar told them the chamber was hexagonal in shape and rose vertically for nearly two hundred feet and dropped below almost half a mile.

"Keep going," Orr said.

They passed through more sediment and entered a circular tunnel on the other end. Bell was starting to sweat inside his suit now. The anomaly had to be just ahead. The magnetometer was reading nanoteslas of incredible intensity. It was as if someone had put the mother of all electromagnetic generators down there. And maybe, just maybe, they had.

The tunnel went on and on and there was no more mindless, silly chatter. This was business now. It took them another fifteen minutes to get through the tunnel and this opened into an immense elliptical antechamber that was something like a thousand feet in circumference at its widest point, sonar told them. Their halogens only penetrated maybe fifteen feet into the clotted murk. It was like moving through a sandstorm at times. From far below, a colony of tubeworms were a forest of pale, rubbery stalks. There had to be hundreds if not thousands of them.

"Like a sea of arteries," Murphy said.

The tubeworms were hollow, about as big around as baseball bats, swaying from side to side. They grew up from twenty feet below and rose fifteen feet above their heads.

"Don't get lost in there," Javonivic said.

They were proceeding by sonar alone now. On the other side of the chamber there was a large oval passage and beyond that, somewhere, the anomaly itself. Using the suit jets, they plowed through the tubeworms, disturbing the rumination of vent fish and pulsing eyeless mollusks much like cuttlefish.

The passage.

Although there was no real reason—other than the usual ones—to fear it, as their lights played over it, Bell was seized by a cold, enveloping dread like it was the mouth of a cave leading to the lair of some flesh-eating beast. Both he and Murphy paused just outside of it, hanging there in the sediment. In the lights of Murphy's helmet, Bell could see that he was feeling the same thing.

"All right, girls," Orr said. "What's the hold up?"

"Nothing, sir," Bell told him.

Working his footpad thrusters, he edged forward into the passage, Murphy at his side. The dread did not abate, but deepened. It felt like birds were taking wing in his belly. His breath was coming fast now, his heart pounding. He knew that Orr and Javonivic were picking up his agitated vital signs.

"Take it easy," she said. "Just take it easy."

They pushed through the passage. The walls were clustered with colonies of round sponges and pink wavering anemone tentacles. They passed giant clams and looping mud worms, punched through dense clouds of krill. The tiny shrimplike animals clung to the aluminum shells of the hardsuits, wiggling their feathery legs.

The further they went, the less life there was until there was none at all. Not even a stray crab skeleton in the collected sediment below. Just that passage, dark and smooth-walled, leading on and on.

"You gotta be damn close now," Javonivic said.

They said nothing. Deeper and deeper they went. The passage was narrowing steadily, but was still quite large.

"Hell is that?" Murphy said, stopping.

Bell was seeing it, too.

Coming from farther down the passage was a phosphorescent glow that was lighting up the tunnel. And whatever was making it, it was coming straight at them.

"We got company," Bell said, not bothering to disguise the fear in his voice.

28

GHOSTS

"What the hell is going on down there?" Orr wanted to know.

He waited a minute, another. He could feel his anger and impatience rising. Finally, the radio squawked and Javonivic's voice came through: "I don't know yet, sir. They've run into something. I'm not getting anything from them."

Orr checked the screen on the console. It was blank.

"Video?" he said.

"It's down, sir," she said.

He cussed under his breath. He could feel an ulcer working at his belly with teeth. "Bell? Murphy? Goddammit, what's going on down there?"

A crackling hiss, some static. Nothing else.

Orr felt something tighten inside him. He was not a man who accepted defeat very easily, but, dear God, he'd been waiting for something like this. Something to go terribly wrong. Down there in that damn city…well, it just had to happen.

"You getting vitals, Javy?"

"Aye, sir. Coming in strong and steady. They're alive…just not answering."

"Shit," he said.

Sitting there in the comm room, surrounded by all that cutting-edge technology, he felt completely helpless. Best-case scenario was that they'd track the anomaly, identify it, and set their charges. Get the hell out and get back to the habitat. Then the mission would be at an end. They could take the submersible up to the LSB and the lot of them could go back up to Kharkov. Screw this damn lake. And screw that damn city and all the horrors gestating in its dark belly.

Best case scenario, that was.

"What's going on, sir?" Anderson asked.

"Fuck if I know, son. What you getting?"

Anderson hovered over his console, checking screens. "I'm getting bio-signs just fine, sir. Heart rates up, respiration up...something's going on."

And that something was what Orr did not like. Because something down in Lake Vordog meant anything. Things you couldn't even begin to imagine.

Or wouldn't want to.

There was a sudden bark of laughter over the radio.

Orr nearly fell out of his chair. What the hell?

"Squid," Bell said. "Of all the goddamned things...a school of squid, sir. Bioluminescent squid. Thousands of 'em. We're caught in a blizzard of them."

"So damn bright right now I'm squinting my eyes," Murphy said.

Dammit.

Orr sighed. "I see. In the future, gentlemen, if you don't mind, when I hail you, you fucking answer me, got it? I don't give a shit if Moby Dick is swallowing your asses, you answer. Is that a roger?"

"Aye, sir," Bell said.

"You boys are giving me gray hairs," Javonivic said, the stress apparent under her words.

"Sorry, Javy," Bell said.

"You getting video on this?" Murphy asked.

"Nothing," Orr told them.

"Amazing..." Murphy paused. "Each one is about three-inches long and brighter than a sixty-watt bulb."

"Passing away now," Bell said.

The video feed came back on. Just the tunnel and the murky water, sediment suspended in the beams of their lights.

"All right," Orr said, mopping sweat from his brow. "Continue mission, gentlemen. Let's get this done with."

REVELATION

The city was in Hubbs' head.

It was haunting him.

Calling to him.

He stood in Entry Lock, staring down into the moon pool, dazed and disoriented, not truly sure if he was dreaming or awake, but fearing he was trapped in some netherworld in-between. He was certain that a gigantic eye was staring up at him from the lake, a globular and hypnotic orb. In his mind, he saw himself climbing into his Exosuit, his mouth set, his movements sure, his eyes like polished glass. *No, no, don't do that,* he warned himself, but his voice barely carried even in his own head. The city was calling his name as it had been for days ever since he had found the tunnel of living corpses. He could no longer shut it out. Every time he tried, his head whirled with dizziness and he thought he would fall straight over like a post.

Don't listen to the voices, he kept telling himself. *Do not listen to the voices.*

But he listened all the same as they spoke and whispered, some singing like sirens to induce him to come to them. He could see those many, many, many eyeless faces and shriveled, puckering mouths that opened wide, calling his name in eruptions of bubbles.

As his hardsuit sealed itself around him, he was overwhelmed by an epiphany that made him see and feel and know reality as he had never known it before. The essential nature of the living condition was made known to him as, some said, it was made known to all at the moment of their death. He was plugged into it, cognizant of it, *part* of it and he could not deny its plan for him.

(*it's always been simple, Hubbs, so very simple: you were born to become part of something much larger than yourself, a cosmic all, part of the many, a gleaming, energetic piece of the whole puzzle that nears completion*)

The disembodied voices chattered constantly, echoing through his head, making him think things that were alien to him and making him do things that he knew were not only inherently wrong, but dangerous.

(*don't fight it: please don't fight it*)

(*there is peace and security and beautiful revelation in what is offered, if you deny it there are horrors, the monsters will come for you and they are hungry*)

Yes, it was all so simple and even serene if you accepted what was offered. The alternative was too horrible to contemplate. By the time he realized this, he was in his suit and the winch, which he had set on auto with a five-minute delay, was activated. It swung over and grasped his hardsuit, slowly swinging it over the moon pool and releasing it below.

The comm on the suit was picking up the crackling, static-filled transmissions of the divers, those of Javy in Main Lock, and Orr up in the LSB.

By the time they realized that he alone had figured out the secret of the city, he would be gone. They couldn't stop him. He was being delivered to the city and what waited for him there.

30
HALLOWEEN GIRL

In the control room of the Neptune's Main Lock, Javonivic felt the tension run through her like blood. She sighed and then sighed again. Though she was not a drinker, she could have handled a good stiff belt just about then. And although she was supposed to stay at the command console at all times—at least *someone* was supposed to, not like you could count on Hubbs to do much but brood these days—she snuck away and made for the head. Had to. Her bladder had gotten so full listening, or not listening, to what was going on in the city, that she thought it was going to burst. She jogged over to the head and did what had to be done.

When she got back, the video was still showing the tunnel, lights splashing around. No life whatsoever. Magnetometers were showing magnetism still spiking. God, they were close. So very close now. Bell and Murphy were nervous. Their life signs had stabilized, but she could hear the nervous undercurrent to their voices even over the microwave link.

She thought: *Sure, they're nervous. I'm nervous just listening to them. That city isn't dead. It's alive. It's sentient, just like Hubbs said. Five minutes in there and you feel it.*

Javonivic was a practicing Christian, a Methodist. She believed in God and his Son and the Holy Ghost. But until she had gone into the city, she had not truly believed in ghosts. Ghosts as malignant survivals, that was. But that place was alive with spirits, absolutely crawling with them.

Evil was not a word she used lightly, but the city was evil, pregnant with malevolent energy and when you went inside it, you crossed the threshold and pierced the barrier between the physical world and the psychic—you plugged yourself into the oppressive and harrowing current of that place. You saw things, you felt things, you knew things that you had no business knowing.

And one of the things you knew was that the city, like those who had made it, was not dead. It was a machine, a terrible organic machine that the bogies had built and now, worshipped as a god. She, of course, did not know any of this to be true, but she felt it deep inside and did not doubt the truth of it. The city was conscious. It read their secret terrors and externalized them. And as the anomaly grew stronger and stronger, the very beating heart of it, she knew something was going to happen. She could feel it. Critical mass was approaching and if Murphy and Bell did not shut it down, something perfectly horrendous was going to happen.

If they could shut it down…if, if, if…

Where the hell was Hubbs?

She got on the habitat intercom and hailed him. Nothing. She hailed him again. Still nothing.

On the radio, Murphy was jabbering on about his hometown of Haymarket, Wisconsin, some isolated agricultural burg stuck out in the middle of fields of corn and wheat and rye. It sounded almost idyllic. But you could tell from what he said and the tone of his voice that he hadn't liked the place. The desolation. The claustrophobic old-world way of thinking. How everything was linked to the harvest. How everyone there seemed to be part of it and he'd felt like an outsider. There was almost a silent terror to his words as he recalled it. She wondered why that was.

"Sounds pretty peaceful," Bell said.

"Sure, sure, I guess it is. But that town…hell, it's like…how do I put it? It's like a pretty rock you find in a field. Real shiny and all, but then you kick it over and there's bugs and crawly things worming on the underside. That was Haymarket. Things happened there in the past you wouldn't believe. But nobody ever talked about it. And when we kids would ask about all those weird, creepy scarecrows out in the fields or Sarah Burges, that little girl that disappeared around Halloween, or about all those empty farmhouses out on Bellac Road, we'd get swatted. There was this one story about—"

"Shut up," Bell said.

Silence.

Javonivic felt her stomach pull up into her chest.

They were seeing something. They had entered another large chamber like a cylinder set on its end. The video showed the gloomy water, the shadows created by the beams of the suit lights and spots. Silt raining down that they had stirred up. A blurry shape moved at the very edge of the lights. Bell and Murphy made surprised gasps, trying to bring their lights around to track whatever it was.

The images were jumping and out-of-focus now. The screen went black, rolled, came back up. Javonivic couldn't say what that shape had been…it was obscure, nebulous…but something about it filled her vitals with ice.

"Hell's going on down there?" Orr wanted to know.

The bio-signs from the suits were reading agitation and fear now, stress: rapid heartbeats, increased respiration, rising blood pressure.

Bell tried to speak, but what came out was a choking sound. "Something…there's something here with us."

"Be careful," Javonivic said, but then she had to say something.

"Pan around," Orr told them.

They did and there was that shape again. Video caught it, lost it, then captured it again. The image shook as the divers tried to bring it into focus.

Javy saw it.

Her own vital signs went through the roof.

A little girl.

Incredibly, impossibly, a little girl was standing there, floating in the murk. She was maybe eight or nine, wearing the ragged, gray Halloween costume of a nurse with a blue cape, her scarlet hair flowing around her in the current like kelp. She was terribly pale and her eyes were like black holes drilled into her face. She was smiling and there was something about that smile that was simply obscene. Macabre.

"Jesus H. Christ…you seeing this?" Bell wanted to know.

"I see it," Javonivic admitted. "She's just floating there."

Like a corpse, she was going to add but didn't dare. The girl looked like flesh and blood, but cadaverous, eyes black and depthless. Maybe not just a little girl, but a little girl that had died and brought back with her all the hideous secrets from beyond the grave.

"Murphy?" Bell said. "You see that?"

His voice was breathy and dry. "Yeah...yeah, I see it, all right."

The girl floated there. She held out her pallid arms and opened her hands like she wanted something. Her mouth opened and dozens of those bioluminescent squid came darting out in a cloud, more and more of them. And then a column of rising bubbles erupted around her. And when they were gone, so was she.

"Holy shit," Bell said. *"You people see that?"*

"Yes," Javonivic said, unable to even imagine how absolutely horrifying it all must have been in the city. Her skin was crawling in frigid waves.

There was silence for a time. The divers panned their lights about, but there was nothing to see. Nothing but that chamber and the silt and the moving shadows.

Bell: "Murph? Murph? You okay?"

Murphy: "Yeah, I...yeah."

Bell: "What is it?"

Murphy: "That girl...I know her. That was the girl who disappeared in Haymarket that Halloween. Sarah Burges. It was her, it was really her."

That's his deepest fear, Javy thought. *Something that terrified him so much that he repressed it like I did with Regina. The city knows it.*

"All right, that's enough," Orr said, sounding pissed off, scared, too many things at the same time. "Pack it in. Proceed and plant your charges."

Javonivic desperately wanted to tell the both of them that it was just a hallucination, a mirage, something the aliens had plucked from Murphy's head and used to torment them with. Just an image. A ghost that looked three-dimensional. The city could project such things. It had the power. Same way it could make harmless jellyfish attack Murphy and the same way it could fill your head with weird visions or send some monster to shake the habitat and the same way it had resurrected her mother. But just because it was a hallucination, did not make it any less real.

When she had woken the other night with something touching her, it had felt like a warm human hand. In her dream, anyway. She hadn't told the others about that part. That the hand had felt like that of Kyle Donniger, the boy who'd taken her virginity in the twelfth grade. And then as she came up out of the dream, it had not felt like a hand at all, but the cold entrails of a gutted fish drawn along her cheek.

The physical hallucination was fleeting.

"Move it along," Orr said. "It was a hallucination, that's all."

"A group hallucination, sir?" Murphy put to him.

"I don't give a shit what you saw," he told them, refusing to admit what he had seen himself. "You got a job to do, so get to it. Ignore that stuff. You hear me? Ignore it!"

"Aye, aye, sir," Murphy said and the sarcasm was so thick in his voice you could have sliced it and served it on crackers.

On the screen, the divers were crossing the chamber for another passage on the other side and one, Javonivic was certain, which would bring them to the magnetic anomaly itself. They pushed on, deeper into that morphic womb of nightmares.

31
CATALYST

Orr had a splitting headache.

And it wasn't, for a change, from what was beneath the lake or what maybe had laid claim to the entire goddamn Pole. No, this was stress. Plain, simple stress brought on by helming a mission that was simply beyond anything he had ever known or would ever want to know again. God knew there had been tight spots in his life. Times when he felt so goddamned helpless, he wanted to punch a hole in the nearest wall. But nothing like this.

He watched Anderson studying the console.

Poor kid. Not even twenty-three yet and look at him...hands shaking, stress lines around his eyes and mouth. And his eyes. When he put them on you, they looked like they belonged to a sixty-year old man that had lived too hard and seen too much. Like the eyes of kids in Vietnam. Nineteen going on fifty. Like Orr himself, Anderson was pretty much getting by on caffeine and adrenaline. Not much else. He rarely slept and what sleep he did get was haunted by nightmares that he woke sweating and screaming from. This whole goddamn project, this lake, that city, all of it...it was like some gigantic dry cell battery charged with negative energy and badness. You could only handle so much of it before it burned you from the inside out.

"How you doing, son?" Orr said to the kid.

Anderson offered him a jittery smile. "I'm...I'm okay."

"Sure. Sure, you are. I'm okay, too. And the sooner we get the hell out of here the more okay we're going to be."

"Yeah…yes, sir."

"Suppose when you were going to DeVry, or wherever the hell a guy like you does his training, I don't suppose you ever imagined you'd be sitting in a buoy on a lake beneath a fucking glacier."

Anderson forced a laugh. "No, sir. The ONR never mentioned this kind of thing when they hired me."

"Just hang tight, kid. It's almost done with now."

Orr listened to Bell and Murphy talking over the wire. They weren't as chatty as before. No joking. No jibes. And definitely no humorous sexual banter between Javonivic and Murphy.

They were all stretched pretty tight by that point and there wasn't a drop of good humor or optimism left in them. Orr had seen that little girl same as Javonivic had. But what the hell was he supposed to say? *Yup, looks like a fucking ghost all right. If I were you, I'd haul ass out of there.* No, he couldn't say that. All he could do was urge them forward to get the job done. NSF, ONI, all the backroom power brokers, no…they wouldn't understand if Orr scrubbed the mission now. They would make an example out of him. And he wasn't even worrying much about them yanking his pension, but he didn't want to lose face.

With his divers.

And particularly with himself.

His record was nearly spotless. He'd always done his best and in the face of overwhelming obstacles. He honestly did not care about what his superiors thought. Not at this juncture. But he was worried about what he would think of himself if he pulled the DSU team out before the job was complete. That's what he feared: the loss of confidence and self-respect. Sometimes it was all you had. He had a pretty good feeling that Bell wasn't too happy with him right about then.

But that was too damn bad.

He was a DSU diver. He knew the risks of his job. The awful sacrifices he might be called upon to make. That was life.

Oh, you make it sound so black-and-white, he told himself. *But it isn't and you know it. Love does not come easy to a man like you. But you love the*

Navy. You love the DSU and the DSSP. The Deep Submergence Unit and the Deep Submergence Systems Project are your whole life. And if you love them, you love Javy, Bell, Murphy, and maybe even Hubbs himself a little bit more. Maybe they look at you as a father-figure and maybe they don't, but you know you look at them like your own kids. You picked them for this op. Out of all the DSU personnel, you picked those four because they were the best. They mean everything to you. And you know goddamn well that if you thought it would save them and get them back home again, you'd swim alone into that fucking city with a bomb strapped to your back. Screw self-respect. Screw it all.

Yes, that was it exactly.

What hurt the most was the fact that they might be losing faith in him. That was the blade that cut the deepest. And if something happened to them, he'd never forgive himself. Fuck the DSU, fuck the Navy, and fuck the United goddamn States of America, they were like his own kids and he could not let anything happen to them.

He actually opened his mouth to tell his divers to pull out...but he didn't.

Couldn't.

Because he knew the Navy. And if he and his team didn't get the job done, they'd simply bring in someone who could. And that would be the last he and the team would ever see of the DSU again. He'd be given a desk job somewhere and put out to pasture. They'd be out of the service. Probably end up with the mercenaries of the deep salvage business or welding gas lines at 600 fathoms. Regardless, it would all be over. For him, for them.

These were the things he told himself because it was easier to chew these things over in his mind than think about the real ramifications of not completing the mission. There were very bad things waiting in the wings if they were not successful. Maybe the file in his safe did not spell them out exactly, but there was no doubt of it in his mind.

Goddammit, they had to find the anomaly. Their lives depended on it.

On the screen, the divers were pushing deeper into the tunnel. Sonar was telling them there was a very large chamber on the other side. This was it. Orr knew it and so did they. This was what they had been looking for.

"Sir?" Anderson said. "It's the Neptune."

Orr punched up the channel. "What do you got, Javy?"

"It's Hubbs."

"What about him?"

"I've been calling all over the habitat for him. He isn't answering..."

"And?"

"Sir, he put the winch on auto and went out in his suit. Lights came on my board. By the time I got to Entry Lock, he was already out there."

"Shit," Orr said under his breath.

"Got him on the external cameras, sir," she said.

The image came over the screen. Hubbs was standing there on the baseplate. On the very edge of it, right where the lights began to fade and things started getting very dark.

"What the hell is he doing?" Orr said. "Hail him, Javy!"

"Have, sir. He's not responding. I think he shut down communications."

Orr tried himself. "Hubbs! Hubbs! Hubbs, you goddamn moron, what the hell are you doing out there? You know rules, you know regs...get your ass back in the lock!"

Anderson shook his head. "No dice, sir. Javy's right: he's shut down his network. He's not hearing you."

Orr watched him standing there on the edge of the baseplate. Without warning, he was suddenly propelled out into the darkness. Gone. And the unsettling part was that Orr could not be sure if he propelled himself or something else just grabbed him and yanked him away.

"Sir!" Javonivic said. "No bio-signs! Nothing from the hardsuit!"

"Dead here, too," Anderson said. "No telemetry."

"Should I go after him?" Javonivic wanted to know.

"Negative on that, Javy. Stay on that board. Nobody goes out alone. That's the regs. Hubbs knew that. He's on his own now."

She switched the video feed back to what the suits were seeing. The tunnel was opening now like the mouth of a funnel. Ahead there was blackness, the beams of the lights spearing into it.

"All right," Orr said. "Now we're going to see what the hell this is about."

32

GHOST TOWN

Bell had all kinds of crazy images in his head of what he'd see when they finally reached the source of the magnetic anomaly. Some behemoth alien machine. An extensive industrial site. All kinds of things. But what he saw was definitely not among them. Sonar told them that the chamber before them was roughly circular in shape and had a mean circumference of something like 3,000 feet. Certainly the largest chamber thus far. But that's all it could tell them.

It couldn't account for what was spread out beneath them.

"Fuck is this?" Murphy said. "You seeing this, Javy? You seeing this?"

"Yes," she said.

A town. The ruin of a small town as seen from above.

Here in this godawful city at the bottom of an ancient lake tucked away beneath the glacier...a *town*. It was lying just beneath them in a hollow: streets with houses on either side and lanes fronted by shops. Weeds and kelp grew up amongst them, roofs set with a flowing green moss. And it was lit up down there. Not brightly, but with a sort of phosphorescent shine that let you see everything.

"This can't be," Bell said. "A town...a fucking town? Down here?"

"It's a mirage," Javonivic told them.

And Bell knew she was right. But it was there, right beneath him and as much as he blinked his eyes, it would not go away.

"It can't be what it seems to be," Orr told them. "It's something, but it's not a town. Just look at it. Looks like Shitsplat, Illinois sunk into the weeds."

Bell and Murphy hovered over it with their jets, moving slowly forward, panning with their cameras and getting a nice panoramic view of the sort that might be seen from a helicopter buzzing a real town. But this one was a desolate graveyard. A weedy run of buildings and rotting houses, shadows pooling from askew doorways, leaning walls encrusted with sponges and flowering anemones, fences lost beneath clustered corals. Brown silt was raining from above, falling over the town like snow. The streets were thick with accumulated sediment, the sidewalks buried beneath the skeletons of crabs and shrimp and the mounded shells of bivalves. The storefronts and porches were barnacled and lumpy.

Many of the buildings had fallen right into themselves and others were nothing but weedy frameworks. The walls of houses were honeycombed with bryozoans, fingers of seaweed growing out of missing windows and doors. There were even cars parked at the curbs, rusted out hulks, skeletal and thick with spiny urchins and moss. Schools of squid abandoned the shell of a church, brittle stars were scattered over rooftops. Many of the houses were gone, nothing but foundations left, basements filled with mud and sea grasses and debris. There were no trees or bushes of the usual sort, but plenty of banks of kelp and seaweed, brilliantly green and red and orange, moving with channels of current like wind through a wheat field.

"Find the anomaly," Orr told them. "It's a mirage, just ignore it."

Bell almost laughed at that. *Ignore it?* How the hell were they supposed to do that? As they moved over the top of it, the ruined town seemed to go on and on. He saw children's sandboxes filled with scuttling crabs. Porch swings that were swollen with some kind of weird red fungus like puffballs about to spore. Silvery eel-like fish swam through gaping holes in the walls of houses. Sea slugs inched over the furry tops of picnic tables.

"That's...Jesus, that's Haymarket," Murphy said as they passed the ulcerated steeple of a church that looked like a broken, leprous finger. "That's my hometown...that's Haymarket, Wisconsin."

Of course it is, Bell thought then. *The aliens pulled it from his mind because they knew the town of his youth disturbed him. So they recreated it here in the weeds...they brought it to life the way Murphy had always envisioned it: a rotting, stagnant corpse.*

"Proceed," Orr said. "I don't want you looking at that place."

"He's right," Javonivic said. "The longer you look at it, the more real it's going to become."

Bell was going to object, and on what grounds he was not exactly sure, but that's when he began to realize that they were right. The longer you looked, the more real it did become. But not in the way they thought. Because at first the town was rough-looking, decayed, abandoned...now it was overgrown with weeds and marine animals so that the houses and buildings were beginning to look almost like Chia pets. The longer they looked, the more it began to resemble some waterlogged corpse on a seabed.

And that's when he saw something else.

There were people down there.

Standing in the streets and leaning out of doorways, others rising up from the weeds. Sarah Burges was one of them. There was an entire population amongst the growths: puffy, pulpy-looking things, bloated and white and worm-holed. They were staring up at the divers. Their mouths opened and closed like the mouths of fish, tiny squid coming out in clouds like cartoon balloons. Pink tendrils wriggled from eyes like tentacles. Mud worms crawled from holes in their chests and bellies.

"Don't look at them!" Javy nearly screamed over the wire.

But Bell couldn't help himself. The bodies were distending, swelling... then, one by one, they exploded, releasing millions of tiny yellow spores. The girl looked up at them, began rising from the town, holding out her fat white fingers to them...and erupted into a cloud of inching green worms.

Bell and Murphy both made strangled cries and hit the thruster footpads in their suits, carrying them over the town that was sinking into the weeds beneath them and into the blackness beyond. A blackness that was darker than anything they'd ever seen before.

"The anomaly," Bell said. "I see it."

33

THE INHABITANT OF
THE CITY

It was there, opening up right before them: the source of the magnetic disturbance itself.

Murphy said, "It's...it's a whirlpool..."

"God, like a black hole," Javonivic said over the wire, her transmission breaking up. "Unbelievable."

They were both right. Or nearly.

It *was* a whirlpool of sorts. A magnetic whirlpool, a self-augmenting matter/energy vortex and about as close to a black hole as you could get without collapsing the mass of a supernova to achieve your ends. To the naked eye, it looked like an immense, cyclical funnel of darkness whose mouth had to be three or four hundred feet across, the water before it and around it, agitated, boiling with random spouts of bubbles.

The vortex was utterly black...but not the murky, grainy blackness of the lake itself, of deep water untouched by light. This was different. A fluid, pulsing blackness that looked much different than the water around it—heavier, denser, gelatinous even. It was rotating slowly like water being sucked down a drain. Now and again, it would flare with occasional spectral shifts of incandescent color: reds, blues, a blazing spike of orange. It reminded Bell of those spinning paint cards at the county fair when he was a kid. The card would spin and you'd dribble paint onto it and it would spray over the card in brilliant abstract patterns. These flares of color were like that. As if something had been dropped into it and instantly atomized.

This is their technology, their science, he thought, dizzy at the sight of it. *Not machines and cumbersome hardware, but the pure cosmic technology of the universe itself, the mechanics of the stars. Not only can they manipulate biology, but matter and space and time.*

"Stars," Murphy said. "I see stars in it."

Yes, Bell saw them, too. Now and again, the vortex would shift, sputter and flare like a solar furnace, giving a glimpse of an impossibly distant sidereal reality of clustered stars.

Orr said something, but it was lost in the rising static. He tried again: "You better arm those charges and get the hell out."

Bell almost started laughing.

The charges? The RDX Comtac? Sure, they had lugged those metal boxes with them. Each about the size of a footlocker, they contained enough hybrid explosives to level three or four city blocks. But looking at that whirlpool, he knew they were not enough. Even a hydrogen bomb would have been useless against this. It was just too far beyond earthly technology. This was like trying to extinguish a star with a firehose.

Around the spherical boundary, there was a bright white ring of agitated atoms and superhot plasma. Now and again, a seething jet of blue matter would come spitting out of the vortexual field and break apart into tiny indigo particles that would spin away through the water in roiling columns of bubbles. Bell figured those particles were hot as the guts of a star and if you got in the way, they'd burn right through you.

Javonivic tried to say something, but it was entirely broken up. But there had been desperation in the few words that Bell had heard that made him try to raise her. It was no good, though. He couldn't raise the Neptune or the LSB now. There was nothing but a whining static on his headset and he had a pretty good idea that it had everything to do with the whirlpool.

"We're moving," Murphy said over the intercom.

It was true.

Maybe that's what she had been trying to warn them about. Because without engaging the vertical or horizontal thrusters of the hardsuits, they should have been sinking. But they weren't. They were held aloft in some kind of neutral buoyancy. And not only that, but they were very gradually moving towards the whirlpool itself.

It was sucking them in.

Like a real black hole, it was cycling in matter, energy, and even light. The exterior suit lights created a field of illumination around them, but the spots they had directed at the whirlpool itself were not acting like light beams normally did. Instead of striking a surface, reflecting off it or being absorbed by it, the beams were bending at right angles as they neared the mouth of the vortex. Bending and being broken up into prismatic rays and sucked deep into the whirlpool itself.

"Shit!" Bell said. *"Shit!"*

Warning lights and buzzers were ringing off in his Exosuit, telling him of impending damage to not only the communication systems, but life support and propulsion as well. Massive electromagnetic radiation leaking from the whirlpool was going to short the suit right out, seize up relays and fuse circuits and shut the onboard computers right down.

"Back! Back!" Bell said.

Both Murphy and he jettisoned the RDX Comtac boxes from their tethers and the boxes drifted away from them, immediately sucked into the vortex. Once they were pulled in, they particulated into brilliant eruptions of matter. The vortex atomized them and would probably put them back together on the other side...wherever that might be.

The thrusters were working, edging them back, but even at full bore it wasn't quite enough. Bell could see by the spicules of silt around him, like a great storm of pollen grains, that they were still being drawn in. The thrusters couldn't put out enough force to cancel the suction of the spinning field. It was like swimming against a riptide. They were not being pulled in quickly, but slowly, very slowly like ants caught in running tree sap.

It was at this time, that Bell became aware of a great, booming vibration that was rising in intensity, shaking both Murphy and he with each resonating thud. Though he could not hear what it was, only feel the vibrations, each thud was like the beat of some immense heart. It pounded through the suit, made the column of the water jar with each beat.

He was facing away from the vortex now, squeezing every drop of power from the thrusters. Murphy had turned around to look. Bell caught sight of his face behind his view plate…it was agonized, terrified. He was screaming out of primal terror.

Don't look! Dear God, don't turn and look…

Murphy was yanked from Bell's side, spinning end over end like a man caught in a free fall, sucked into a vacuum, pulled into the vortex and there wasn't a damn thing he could do about it. He screamed himself hoarse, but it was pointless.

In the center of the whirlpool, there was a steadily growing silver disk that shimmered and rippled. It looked like the surface of a mirror or maybe a window. And through it, the Old Ones. Not one or two, but a hundred. A thousand. Ten thousand. Like a swarm of glossy gray-black beetles taking wing, they filled that window which looked into some dead-end of space, a place so distant that it probably wasn't even calculable by conventional mathematics. The Old Ones filled that window, distorted and fluttering, more pressing in all the time.

And then the image went black and that blackness split right open.

It split lengthwise and something started to slither out in a churning polluted mist of flickering colors. It was hideous and gigantic, flesh and smoke and steel mist. A spiraling thermonuclear furnace that was alive, a biological profusion that was burning and smoldering, its guts filled with writhing crystalline entrails that were dissolving into steam and gushing fire. A polychromatic nuclear chaos, a noxious creeping fungus set with leering yellow eyes like suns going supernova and a million undulating tentacles of translucent, energized tissue coiling and squirming and spreading out into a living forest of feelers. Like the abomination itself, they were composed of searing radioactive plasma, crystallized yet fluid, flesh but smoke. The thing came on, revealing more and more of itself in the strobing, radiant fire-storm of its own blazing anatomy.

Bell went nearly mad at the sight of it.

Something shattered inside him like white ice as he felt himself being drawn towards that anti-dimensional horror. He shook with involuntary spasms inside his hardsuit as if he were a hatchling trying to break free from an egg. Hot and cold sweat poured from him in rivers. He pissed himself. He vomited bile. And through it all, he managed to see Murphy get sucked in. He hit the vortex and the entire thing rippled, the image of that monstrous entity shivering. He was broken apart into a violent spray of colors as he was particulated.

And that's when Bell knew that that entity was not close at all, probably miles distant, but so vast it filled the vortex.

A shockwave passed from the whirlpool and the water surged around him. The thrusters grabbed. There was a momentary displacement in the field, an interruption, and it was enough for him to pull away deeper into the chamber.

The vortex faded behind him.

And then, through the drifting silt, he passed over the outer edges of where the town must have been, Murphy's town. But it wasn't there. Below, there was a wavering field of luminous marine growths.

He was going to make it.

He told himself that he would indeed make it.

If the suit would hold out, if the batteries still had enough charge to get him back to the SDV outside the city. It was a long way, but he would make it. If the Exosuit's systems could just hold up until he got to the SDV. That's all he would need. The back-up systems had like forty-eight hours of emergency life support.

The microwave net brought nothing but static. He cancelled it out, his head filled with a roaring sound. The city itself was silence: the thousand-mile silence of a moonlit summer night. A hive of shadows and shapes and stark memory bunching in black fibers. And—

Dear God, what was that?

The radio was off. He could not have heard anything in that city, in that stygian lake, and particularly through the reinforced shell of the hardsuit. But he *was* hearing something. Echoes that bounced around him, through him.

And music.

It wasn't possible, but he was hearing it…tinny, distant music like the shrilling of a carnival calliope carried by an August night breeze. It grew louder and louder until he wanted to press his hands to his ears to shut it out. But that would do no good and he knew it. Because it was in his head: a reedy piping that was scratching and dissonant, yet musical and rhythmic. The obscene trilling of a million strident grasshoppers that were the voices of those who had built the city. And not two or three, but dozens and dozens, all piping away madly with that melodious, symphonic fluting that was ear-piercing and manic.

And from the luminous weeds below, they rose up.

The Old Ones.

Thirty or forty or fifty or sixty, they soared up and encircled him like a great swarm of late-season crane flies, spreading their wings, tentacular walking legs coiling and limbs twitching and those brilliant red eyes looking at him and *into* him, owning him and filling him and ultimately crushing him. Their carapaces were gray and black and metallic blue. More and more emerged, fanning out like waves until there was a solid wall of them closing in around him. And those eyes. All those eyes eating into him like acid.

And in his helmet, there was a buzzing/piping noise that grew louder and louder and louder, a chanting, insectile imitation of human voices all shrieking in his head: *Bell, Bell Bell, Bell, BELL, BELL, BELL, BELL, BEEEELLLLLLLLLL-*

On and on until it was a white sibilant noise that became the whining screech of buzzsaws and his skull cracked open like a soft egg.

And Bell was gone.

His head came apart in a Technicolor blur of meat and tissue, blood and gray matter spraying in wormy loops against the inside of the clear bubble of his view plate.

The lights on his suit winked out one by one.

And he sank like a brick into the oily blackness far below.

EPIC FAIL

Javonivic hadn't heard from the LSB in over forty-eight hours now. Bell and Murphy were surely dead.

She was alone.

Isolated.

Helpless.

Part of her thought that Hubbs was behind it, but he had been gone for days and there was no way he could have docked his suit out of the moon pool without triggering alarms. The more she thought about it the less she was convinced that Hubbs had anything to do with it whatsoever. He was probably dead. His hardsuit had eight hours of life support with forty-eight hours emergency backup…but that would have been cutting it pretty close.

It's not Hubbs and you know it, she told herself. *He's dead. They're all dead. Probably Orr and his tech above, too, and maybe even the boys up in the drill tower. And you know damn well who or what is behind it.*

She did. But it was the *how* and *why* that concerned her. Why would the Old Ones kill the others and leave her alive? What would the point be? To toy with her? To study her? To see what happens to the human mind when it begins to disintegrate?

Then she stopped. She would not give the bogies the enjoyment of thinking they had beaten her. Maybe they had, but she would never admit it.

Options.

She sat at the computer console and weighed them out. First off, even though she could not raise the LSB, what she saw on her screen told her that not only was the buoy still up there, but it was still functioning. She was still getting electricity and freshly-scrubbed oxygen from the generators and compressors up there. So no need to panic just yet. If that failed, she could go on emergency life support in the Entry Lock, pressurize it independently. That would buy her time. The microwave telemetry system was offline and so were video, audio, and data connectivity.

Good and bad.

There was always her hardsuit.

Yes, the Exosuit!

She could climb into it and ascend to the surface...but if no one was there, no one was alive on the LSB, then what? The ADS hardsuits were fantastic in the water, but out of it they were bulky and heavy, weighing over a thousand pounds. She would need somebody to winch her out of the water. There was no auto winching like on the habitat. If she surfaced, she would just bob around like a drum.

Emergency release, dummy!

Yes, of course. Why the hell wasn't her head working right? The Exosuits had emergency release systems. If you were in danger or couldn't get the suit off, you could override life support and the suit would open to release the pilot. You had to enter preset coordinates to do it, though. The whole process was complicated and necessarily so, otherwise a pilot might jettison his suit at the bottom of the sea accidentally.

"Well," she said out loud, beginning to feel a bit of the old self-confidence welling up in her. "Maybe my goose isn't cooked quite yet. Seasoned, but not ready for the pot."

That's what she would do. Ascend to the LSB, jettison the suit and climb aboard. Then, if Orr and his techie were dead or gone, she would contact the tower. And if that wouldn't work, she would activate the cable car that was completely automated. It would drop down and up she would go.

Unless that technology failed her, too.

Because things were definitely not right. She could not seem to find a reason why the microwave net was down. Why all the emergency communications systems were inoperable. It was like they had been sabotaged. The Neptune module was supplied with air and power, had food and water for another month...but was essentially cut off. Now why was that?

Maybe she didn't want to know.

And the thing was, she did not really trust herself to figure such things out.

Her brain was not operating at peak efficiency. She was making mistakes. And she had been ever since losing contact with Bell and Murphy. That had been the time for action. The time to switch to full-blown survival mode and get out. But what did she do? After losing contact with Bell and Murphy, she lost contact with the LSB, then she just sat at the console in the control room and...waited. Waking. Sleeping. But never leaving. For eight hours she had done that. Then she took a few Darvocet and laid down in her bunk.

But why?

Why had she done that?

She knew protocol, she understood procedure. You didn't make it in the DSU if you didn't. But for two days she had done nothing but sleep and eat, lost in some fugue. And the more she thought about it, the more she began to wonder if that fugue was not artificial and she had been placed in it by some external agency that did not want her to leave.

It was only since waking a few hours ago that her head seemed to be working.

What the hell had happened?

What if the escape pods had not been fired by the bogies, but by her? Panicking now, uncertain of what was real and what was not, she brought up the screen for the the escape pods. They had ascended at 11:23 p.m. last night. She had no memory of where she had been or what she had been doing. She began to wonder if maybe while she thought she had been in some mindless fugue, she had actually been sabotaging her own survival.

Was that possible?

She knew it was. The bogies could make you see things that were not there. They could make you do things and believe things that were wholly erroneous. And she did not doubt that they could easily manipulate your mind in other ways, too.

To hell with it…what did it matter?

She was getting out of here.

And she was getting out before anymore goddamn mind games were played on her. DSU divers were survivors. They were trained to meet and overcome any and all obstacles. She let that training take over now and never was she was so relieved to be a brainwashed little automaton. She went over to the diving suit storage racks. Her suit was there along with two back-ups. She chose her own. Like the others, it was meticulously maintained. She went through the drill. Batteries fully charged. Primary and auxiliary life support operational. Propulsion ready. Navigation equipment on-line. Hull integrity secure.

The suit was fully operational.

And so was she.

She climbed up onto the step and began to work her way into the suit.

There was a sudden beeping.

She almost came right out of her skin. The winch had been activated. It slowly swung out over the moon pool. Only an incoming diver could activate it like that.

What the hell?

She checked the security cameras. They showed no diver or anything else below or at the perimeter of the platform. The winch was in position. She had to override it, she had to—

Shit.

The feed on the external security cameras was not live. It was merely spooled data feed from two days ago. Why the hell hadn't she noticed that? She had some vague recollection of watching Hubbs when he left the habitat that day. Watching that same tape footage again and again. And it was still replaying it. She canceled the feed and brought up the outside of the habitat. Nothing. Just static. The cameras were down. As were the external motion detectors, sonar grid, and even the thermals.

Jesus, all of it was dead.

With a cry scraping from her throat, she raced for the winch controls. The clamp was dropping down into the moon pool. But it wasn't too

late. It couldn't be too late. She punched the override controls. *Nothing.*
She punched them until her fingers ached. Still nothing. She threw the
emergency shut-off. A warning light flashed again and again.

MALFUNCTION

MALFUNCTION

MALFUNCTION.

She hammered the override buttons. No good. The clamp was still
descending.

"What the fuck is going on here?" she shouted as she kept punching the
buttons.

She knew she had to relax.

But there were only moments now before the winch brought the suit
up. It could have been Hubbs. In fact, the screen told her that it *was* Hubbs.
His suit was sending telemetry, but no biosigns. She punched a channel
through. "Hubbs?" she said, her voice breaking in her throat. "Hubbs?
Hubbs, is that you?"

The clamp had been activated.

The winch was bringing it back up.

"Hubbs! Hubbs!" Javonivic screamed into the mic. *"Hubbs! Hubbs!
Goddammit, Hubbs…is that you?"*

No reply.

Just static. A static with some eerie humming sound buried in it. Every
muscle in her body was bunched in sheer animal terror. Her nerves were
electrified and jarring. Her heart was pounding. Her scalp pierced by
needles.

A weapon.

*Find a weapon. You're a fucking DSU diver, you silly little bitch! Protect
yourself! Find a weapon!*

Gasping for air in full-blown panic mode now, she grabbed a speargun.
Oh yes, that would work. She saw a propane torch. It would shoot out a
five-foot flame. Now her head was working. Start with that. If worse came
to worse, she could run into the Main Lock, depressurize Entry.

The clamp was coming up.

Weapons in hand, shaking and nauseous with a fear that actually
burned in her guts, she stood ready on the wet porch. The winch was

spooling back in. For all intents and purposes, it was working. But she knew it wasn't working. Nothing was working. Everything had gone insane and she wasn't far behind.

The clamp brought Hubb's Exosuit up out of the moon pool.

35
ORGANISM

Javonivic was so scared now her guts were shriveling with fear. There was a hollow booming sound in the back of her head. She wanted to scream. To run. The suit was up all the way now and the MALFUNCTION light was no longer blinking. She dove at the controls, dropping the speargun, and thumbing the override. It worked. Her breath barely coming now, a moaning in her throat, she threw the emergency shut-off. It held. The winch was dead. The suit just hung there from the clamp like a marionette with no one working its strings. Water ran from it. The legs and arms were moving slightly.

She calmed a bit.

Whoever was in there, they were going nowhere. She had them.

She punched up a channel again. "Hubbs," she said, trying to keep the panic from her voice. "If you're in there...tell me so. You have exactly one minute. If you don't, I'm going to take this propane torch and cook you in your suit. I swear to God I will...*I'm not fucking around here.*" Tears ran from her eyes, her voice cracking with sobs. "Don't test me...whatever in the fuck you are, don't you dare test me."

There was nothing but that static from the suit.

"All right then."

Taking up her speargun and torch, she went over to the wet porch. She was within seven feet of the suit now. Whoever was in there was still dangling, limbs moving sluggishly. Using her foot, she turned the spotlights on the suit...and instantly recoiled in horror.

It was not a man.

Through the helmet view plate, she could see something like a face, but one that was white and pulpy and blown-up to fantastic proportions. It actually filled the helmet, pressing up against the glass. She saw oozing, puffy flesh, great flabby lips, and eyes that were not eyes, but gelatinous things like scarlet comb jellies.

Then she did scream.

The suit was trembling. The view plate cracked.

It split open and white flesh oozed out like congealed fat. The aluminum hull of the suit began to squeal as it underwent intense pressure from within. It was forged aluminum and could take crushing pressure... but nothing like this. It began to expand with a shrill metallic whine of metal fatigue. Great baseball-sized lumps popped in its shell. Dozens of them. Then it sheared right open, popping like a tube of biscuits when you pull the cardboard wrapper or press a spoon to the seam...it burst open and that gelid white monstrosity poked out from a dozen places like dough.

Javonivic got her first real look at what was inside.

If it was Hubbs, then he had been infested and parasitized by morbid marine growths, becoming a bloated, spongy excrescence in the shape of a man. It dangled there from the rent hardsuit, expanding, dilating, pushing ever outward.

Javonivic could see things that were trapped in the pulsing mass—tiny transparent squid and brine shrimp, copepods and squirming ectoparasites. And the most horrifying thing was that somehow, some way, it still resembled a man. One inflated to incredible proportions, boneless and protoplasmic, yet gruesomely man-shaped: limbs moved and fingers wiggled, a great flabby mouth like that of a grouper pealed back in a sneer, and the eyes—like candied, sticky cherries running with syrup—still blinked and looked at her.

She pulled the trigger of the speargun.

There was a swishing noise as the spear shot out and sank into the central mass with a wet thud. The thing continued to grow and swell, the spear lodged in its midsection, for all the good it did. As she watched, the spear began to slash side to side as if something in there was gripping in it.

She let out a mad, wailing sound that rushed scream-like from her throat. Not daring to take her eyes off the thing, she fumbled with the propane torch. Those red, juicy eyes staring back at her expanded until they popped like bubbles. And the thing continued to bulge and increase, huge tears ripping open in its hide, revealing something beneath like the rubbery skeleton of a gorgonian. She caught but a glimpse of it and then those gaping holes were filled with coiling things and corkscrewing things—the feeding tendrils of soft mushroom coral, bristleworms and fanworms, the radial arms of crinoids. And then it became an immense writhing aggregation of pale-yellow marine polyps, bursting with thousands of pink stinging tentacles like those of deep-sea anemones. They undulated in the air, thousands of them, stubby and clutching, like human fingers.

And Javy knew that if she didn't burn it there and then, it would drop into the water and slither up from the moon pool and devour her, absorb her, do things she did not even want to imagine.

She opened the valve on the propane tank, lit the flame.

The thing trembled with fluttering rhythmic vibrations as if it knew what she was about to do. She opened the valve and a blue-white tongue of flame reached out for that grotesque mass and found it. It made a weird, high-pitched squealing sound as it tried to free itself from the remains of the suit which was like some ruptured egg that had given it birth. The multitude of pink tentacles stabbed out blindly, whipping through the air, scooping and fanning, trying to find something to grab.

But she swept the guttering flame back and forth over it, tentacles withering and blackening, curling up. Burning and letting out gouts of vile-smelling smoke, the creature continued to whine, engulfed in flames. Finally, it clutched like a fist, charred and smoldering, and went still. It dangled there from the Exosuit in pouches and ribbons and flaps of burnt tissue…then it dropped from the suit and fell into the water, sizzling a moment before sinking entirely. It left a greasy oil slick to mark its passing.

Javonivic turned off the valve and dropped the propane tank.

She stumbled back two or three feet and promptly went down on her ass. Her vision swam and her head was filled with a dull thundering noise.

She sat there, breathing in and out, shivering with the delayed reaction of absolute shock.

Slowly, she crawled to the Main Lock hatch. She opened it and stepped through. She heard the shrilling of the sonar alarm. *It's not working! It's all in your head!* Regardless, she made it to the console and saw a huge blip approaching the triangle of the habitat. It was the same size and shape as the one that had that attacked them and stripped away the submersible.

No, no, no, not again, dear Christ, not again.

(ALICE I'M COMING)

Javonivic let out a cry. Not Regina. No, not that thing. Not that horror. She didn't have the strength to fight against it now.

(ALICE DO NOT TURN AWAY FROM YOUR MOTHER)

Javy shook her head from side to ride. It was not real. None of it could be real. She had to force it from her head, but as she tried, the strength of what had invaded her mind swelled until it filled her skull.

(ALICE)

(LOOK AT ME ALICE)

(I AM YOUR MOTHER LOOK AT ME)

Javy, tears rolling down her face, found herself walking to one of the viewports. She had no will of her own. The monstrosity that was Regina worked her like a puppet and she blindly shambled forward with spasmodic strides.

Oh Christ, oh Jesus Christ...

(LOOK UPON YOUR MOTHER)

(ONLY I LOVE YOU)

(ONLY I)

She saw an agitated, boiling storm of bubbles and a maelstrom of conflicting currents swirling in some great, churning whirlpool, an immense white mass born from it that opened like a fist, unfurling gigantic white tentacles that reached out for the Neptune.

And then the entire habitat began to shake.

CHAOS

The LSB was under attack.

Orr was not in his right mind. In fact, he felt like he was lost somewhere south of where his mind should have been. Time had become fluid. He could remember little of the past few days in which Anderson and he waited and waited to hear from the habitat in vain. There were things he should have done. He was in charge. This was his operation. Yet, he had only waited, seemingly watching himself do nothing, shouting at himself to take action.

There was a way to end this, he thought as the LSB rolled with turbulence. *You know what it was and what it is. You have the codes.*

Anderson was curled up in the corner, covering his head as the LSB groaned and shook, hatches blowing open, computer screens exploding with showers of sparks and smoke. Rivets popped from the walls. A chair from across the room flew through the air and slammed into a bulkhead.

The cable car. You need to activate it before it's too late if it's not already.

He climbed to his feet and the deck beneath him rumbled, rolling with a shockwave that tossed him back down. He fought forward, the air filled with smoke and a perfectly sickening smell of burnt wiring and melted plastic. He took hold of Anderson who was a trembling bag of bones. Yanking him none too gently to his feet, he pulled him through the door out onto the deck.

One of the lights out there exploded with a flash of blue light. The ROV was thrown from its cradle, splashing into the lake, the waters of which seemed to be boiling, hissing with plumes of steam and rolling clouds of dirty mist. A winch made a shrill squealing sound and broke free of its stanchions, crashing to the deck. A high-voltage line exploded and began to burn.

Enough.

Goddamn enough.

Leaving Anderson, he dashed into the command room and activated the cable car. The readouts told him that it was beginning its descent.

Anderson let out a cry and Orr ran back out there. He saw what paralyzed the boy with fear—something was rising from the water in a flurry of bubbles.

37
BORN AGAIN

Far below, the Neptune not only shook, it vibrated.

It trembled.

It began to roll first one way, then the other as if it was hit by a seismic wave. Javonivic was tossed to the floor, thrown across the room. The habitat groaned and creaked. One of the hardsuits fell from its bracket. The propane tank rolled passed her and dropped into the moon pool. Warning lights were flashing. Sirens shrilling. The lights flickered, went out, plunging her into absolute blackness. Then the back-ups came on. The integrity of the structure had been weakened. The passage between the Main and Entry Locks was sealed off with a hiss of air.

Entry Lock was losing compression.

Water was spraying everywhere now from burst seams and popped rivets. It was like a dozen showerheads were turned on full blast. There were clouds of moisture and steam in the air.

Javy scrambled to her feet.

(I AM HERE ALICE)

She would not listen. She would not hear the voice. If she listened, she would go mad. Utterly and completely mad.

The computer terminals were dead. The moon pool was gushing and bubbling as the water level rose, the air leaking away. Through one of the tiny viewports, she could see a flurry of rising bubbles. She raced over to the life-support controls, trying to override the emergency procedures that had sealed off the passage. She had to get back into the Main Lock, one way or another.

She had but minutes and she knew it.

No dice. Life-support computers had discovered a breach in Entry Lock's hull causing loss of compression and they did what they were designed to do: contain the atmosphere in Main Lock. It was either climb into one of the Exosuits and take a chance or open the emergency crawlway between the locks. She had less than five minutes to do so before it, too, was permanently sealed off.

Panicking, she stood there precious seconds, frightened, confused.

If she escaped into the Main Lock, she was trapped until life support ran out. But if she clambered into one of the suits and got trapped in the Entry Lock, she would die there, too.

C'mon, girl! Don't freeze up now! This is where you separate the men from the boys and the women from the little girls! Think! Act! You've been through the drills! Do something!

She knew there was no choice.

The water rushing up around her knees, she went over to the winch and powered it up. It worked. Thank God. She released the clamp, dropping the wrecked Exosuit into the water where it filled and sank out of sight. She swung the winch back and clamped her own suit, set the auto-drop feature.

There. That wasn't so hard.

The water was up to her hips now.

The warning lights were still flashing, the sirens and buzzers shrilling so loudly that she could barely think. The moon pool and wet porch were invisible beneath the rising torrent of water. Great gurgling bubbles rose up. She reached for her suit.

(NOW IS THE HOUR OF YOUR DESTINY)
(LISTEN TO YOUR MOTHER'S VOICE)

The habitat was hit again.

And again.

Javonivic was tossed into the water, swept this way and that. She smashed up against a bulkhead, then was pulled away in the direction of the moon pool. The water there was gushing and foaming, a great whirlpool forming and drawing everything towards its epicenter like the drain of a tub. Air tanks and water bottles, life vests and swim flippers, lengths of hose and mylar-covered operations manuals…in fact, everything that was not tied down was being pulled towards the effervescing eye with incredible suctioning force.

Javy included.

(ALICE)

(I'M COMING FOR YOU ALICE)

Javy tried to grab hold of things, bulkheads and steel racks and benches bolted to the deck plates, but everything was slick and greasy. The whirlpool was rotating her around and around and she could not get her bearings. The alarms whined in her ears, water sprayed in her face. She was a trained swimmer, sleek and well-muscled and athletic. She fought with everything she had until her limbs felt like lead, but it was no good.

Exhausted, defeated, she fought no more.

The maelstrom spun her around and around in ever-decreasing circles. She would be sucked down and drowned and maybe, in the final analysis, that wasn't such a bad thing after all.

She kept her head above water but that was about it. She was tapped and weary, both physically and psychologically. The water sluiced and foamed and she accepted her end. And then, just as she neared the epicenter and felt the tidal pull from below, the whirlpool ceased and water was not drawn out of the Entry Lock, but forced into it. A tidal wave of force came from below and she was suddenly riding a column of water that dashed her against a bulkhead and sank her into the depths.

She lost consciousness for a few seconds maybe and came up, gasping for air, shaking the water from herself. The suction was gone, but the water was still rising. It was up to her chest now. A hardsuit went floating by like a corpse. There was bobbing debris everywhere. And the Neptune itself… or at least the Entry Lock…was leaning precariously to one side. Either the baseplate itself had been ruptured or one of the support legs beneath was badly damaged.

But, dear God, she thought then, *what could possibly have hit the habitat with enough force to jar one of the legs? Each of them weighs over six tons…*

And maybe the answer would have come to her, but that's when she realized that she was not alone in the flooding Entry Lock. Something had come up out of the moon pool from below.

Shit.

Something brushed against her and she let out an involuntary cry.

She caught a glimpse of some serpentine and almost phosphorescently white object in the water with her. And whatever it was, it was damn big and damn quick, easily the size of a monstrous python. There were many of them, she soon saw, in front of her, looped around behind her, filling the water like some peristaltic tangle of worms, immense and obscenely fleshy.

The first thing she thought, almost abstractly, was: *sea snakes.*

It was ridiculous, of course, down here in this primordial lake beneath the glacier. But that was her first impression. There was a school of sea snakes in the water with her.

Her second impression was a little closer to the truth: *tentacles.*

She saw them. And if for one fleeting moment she had been thinking anything as prosaic as squid or octopus, she knew better now. No earthly, ordinary cephalopod had tentacles like this. They were white, shiny, rubbery, and flattened out like oars. And she was lost in a forest of them. They bumped her. Nudged her. Whisked against her legs. Some were two- and three-feet across, others were the size of her arms or legs. And they just kept coming, more and more and more of them until they not only filled the water, but rode up out of it in spirals and undulant loops. It was like being trapped in a nest of mating vipers. She did not even want to think of what they might be connected to.

Please, oh please, Lord above, help this sinner, help this poor lost soul in my final—

(STOP IT ALICE)

(YOU CANNOT PRAY)

(YOU WERE BORN WITHOUT A SOUL)

But that was wrong, oh, it was so wrong. She wasn't like her mother, she was not at all like Regina, who, at that ugly moment, was filling her head with images and ancestral memories that she plucked from the depths of Javy's own mind, informing her and schooling in this final hour.

(IT IS THE WOMAN THAT SPAWNS LIFE IN THESE GREEN DEPTHS)

"No! Leave me alone! Get out of my head!"

The horror and repulsion that filled her was organic and instinctual.

(YOU MUST BREED AND MULTIPLY AND FILL THE DARK WATERS WITH YOUR SPAWN)

One of the tentacles rose up out of the water in front of her like a blind, albino worm. She could see that it had suckers not just in single or double or triple rows like ordinary cephalopods, but seemingly dozens and dozens of them opening and closing like hungry, puckering mouths. They were crowded over the underside of the tentacle. They made smacking sounds like kissing lips as they irised open and closed.

It moved in closer to her, water dripping from it in runnels.

A violent, caustic stench came from it that reminded her of rotting grapes fermented to wine and turpentine-soaked rags. Whatever it was, it made her eyes water and her nose run.

In utter, unreasoning fear, she thought: *I wish it would just kill me. I want to die. I don't want to know about the things it wants to teach me.*

The water was cold. She felt numb as hypothermia settled in. She wouldn't last much longer. Already, her mind was losing focus.

The tentacle in front of her got within spitting distance, the sound of its puckering suckers making her skin crawl. It moved in slowly and she steeled herself for the horrid feel of it. She was shaking. Tears ran down her cheeks. Bile bubbled up the back of her throat. It still had not touched her, but now it was so close that she could see tiny pores or something like pores in its even white flesh. When the suckers opened, there was something pink and squirming in each...like a tongue.

That's what it will taste you with, a hysterical voice in her head cried. *A thousand tongues. A thousand-thousand fat pink tongues—*

It was too much. Something sheared open inside her and she let out a moan of repulsion. She struck out at it with her fists, punching it three or four times in rapid succession. It was very muscular, firm. But instead of attacking her like she thought it would...and maybe hoped it would...it just withdrew, pulling out of striking distance, but not going away.

The water was nearly up to her shoulders now. It still sprayed from ruptured seams, dripped from the roof. She wiped a sheen of it from her face.

Breathing hard, she said, "What do you want from me?"

(ALICE I AM YOUR MOTHER)

No, no, no. She would not listen to it. She would not hear that booming voice and the awful things it said.

(DON'T FIGHT CHILD DO NOT FIGHT)

(WHEN MY TIME CAME, I RETURNED TO THE SEA AS YOU MUST RETURN)

Javy thrashed in its grip, her head shaking back and forth, rejecting what was said inside her mind. Regina was insane. She had always been insane. Frightened. Paranoid. Terrified of the sea, yet she had watched it constantly, fascinated by it and, perhaps, by what waited in its depths.

(YOUR TIME IS NOW)

The tentacles in the water were moving as if excited: bumping and brushing against her, but, again, not in a threatening way. The one before her just hovered there like a confused snake. She didn't want to assume for one moment that something like this had a sentient brain, a soul that understood mercy and compassion and, worse, tenderness…but that's how this thing was acting. It could have taken her at any time, crushed her, fed her to its mouth if it had one, or just licked the skin from her face, but it did nothing. Which meant either it was a gentle soul or it was sadistic, enjoying the torment of its prey.

The tentacle moved in again.

Javonivic tensed.

A cylinder of compressed air floated by. She reached out and picked it up. Something savage in her liked its weight and feel. When the tentacle got within reach, almost investigative like a child's finger, she swung the cylinder with both hands. She hit it again and again until her breath came quick in her lungs and her arms were tired. It did not withdraw. It did not defend itself. It did nothing but accept the beating she gave it. And that was more than confusing, it was infuriating. She had hit it so hard and so many times that she had dented the cylinder and actually chipped paint from it.

"Kill me, goddammit!" she screamed at it. *"I've had enough, you goddamn ugly fucking monster! I've had enough!"*

The tentacles in the water thrummed around her. The one before her came in closer again and this time it moved with incredible speed, whipping out to what she thought would be to take her head right off, but that's not what happened. It slapped the cylinder right out of her hands.

Javy, caught in some hallucinatory netherworld between madness and distorted reality, began to sob. She was not a crier. Moving in a world dominated by men, she had learned to be as tough as them. But now she cried like a scolded little girl, wracked with sobs.

(YOU WERE DRAWN TO THE DEEPS AS OUR KIND ALWAYS ARE)

"No, no, no! It's not true, Mama…it's just not true. I'm not like you. I'm not…oh God, I'm not…"

Maybe twenty-feet away, where the moon pool probably was, there was an eruption of rising bubbles. The water in Entry Lock thrashed with waves and ripples as more of the creature emerged. She found herself looking at a bulging cluster of pods or fleshy bubbles that were roughly formed into some great glistening hood. And near the top were a circle of close-packed green eyes, each larger than a softball. They were moist and gelid. And they blinked in unison, a shiny transparent membrane sliding over them and retreating.

She gasped.

Yes, that was its head and its eyes and somewhere down there was the mouth which would ingest her.

(IN THE END, WE ALWAYS RETURN TO THE SEA)

(IT'S IN OUR BLOOD)

(IT'S OUR DESTINY)

(IT'S OUR HERITAGE)

A roping mass of tentacles nudged her forward, then forward again. Not roughly really, just insistently. She fought and splashed, but there was no denying their strength. She was still crying, still shaking with spasms. Those eyes held her and…fascinated her. They were not evil or predatory, really, just alien and huge and starkly weird. And maybe it was rioting imagination, but they almost looked…intelligent.

Breathing in and out very fast, she said, "Get it over with…I can't take anymore of…this…"

The eyes blinked.

And the tentacles in the water began to move and slither. They pressed in and she could feel them coiling around her under the water. They slid around her legs and waist and belly. This was it. She knew this was it. She'd asked it to kill her and now it was going to grant that final wish.

But the tentacles did not squeeze.

They kept up an even pressure, but one that was not uncomfortable, but almost...reassuring. Like the arm of a loved one looped around you in a time of stress or pain. As if...as if that thing felt her pain and was trying to comfort her. Manic laughter burst in her head at the idea of it. *Regina never comforted me. She hated me. She despised everything I was. I saw murder in her eyes a dozen times.* The tentacles were not cold, but warm and getting warmer. Deliciously warm in the freezing water. Some mad impulse in her almost liked the idea of them wrapping her up.

You're losing your fucking mind!

(NO ALICE YOU ARE BECOMING)

(SOON YOU WILL SWIM IN THE CITY)

"I don't want that...Mama, please, oh please, I don't want that..."

(YES)

(YOU WERE ALWAYS DRAWN TO THE SEA)

(YOU CANNOT ESCAPE YOUR HERITAGE)

The tentacles had been cold, so very cold, but now they were warm. Almost as if they were reacting to her own core temperature. Trying to keep her warm and comfortable.

And the way they pressed against her.

Touching.

Feeling.

Whispering over her flesh.

God, it was like they were...well, caressing her. Warm. Gentle. Welcome. Familiar. The way she had always wanted her mother to be.

Stop it! Stop it! Are you out of your fucking mind? Look at that thing! Good Christ, look at it, will you? It's a horror! A fucking monster from a B-Movie! It doesn't know tenderness or emotion! It eats things! It crushes them! It sucks blood! It lives in a fucking undersea cave full of human bones! Can you doubt that? Well...CAN YOU?

She just wasn't sure.

One of the tentacles slid up between her legs and she thought she would scream. It pushed up with a not uncomfortable pressure. It was warm, then hot as if she was soaking in a bubble bath.

One of the tentacles rose up and brushed against her face.

(THE RABBIT HOLE ALICE)

What? *What?*

(YOU WENT DOWN THE RABBIT HOLE)

(YOU RETURNED TO THE DEEPS)

The borehole. It was talking about the borehole. Like Alice in the children's book, she had gone down the rabbit hole and reality had never been the same again.

The tentacles so warm, so comforting, so soft. She felt the suckers against her cheek, sensed the strength of them and knew they could have sucked the flesh from her bones. But they didn't. The worming pink tongues came out and began to lick her with corkscrewing motions, tracing circles and lines over her face. Their touch was at first offensive like maggots wriggling against her and she knew she should be horrified. Insane with it. But she wasn't. Their touch was sedative, soporific.

The tentacle withdrew.

Swallowing, starting to feel less and less afraid, she looked into those eyes.

They were really very beautiful and she wondered if any human had ever been this close to the creature, to gaze into those amazing translucent eyes. They were the eyes of a monster haunted by its own desolation and loneliness. The shades of green they possessed—emerald and jade, aquamarine and sage, the deep green of pine forests and the bright green of fresh, dewy apples—was astonishing. And more…shades of sea-green and summer moss and almost an indigo. Deep and luscious, chromatic and dazzling, crystalline and multifaceted. There were pigments of green she had never seen before and she wanted to sink into them, swim through them.

(YES ALICE)

(YOUR TIME IS NOW)

(I AM YOUR MOTHER)

"Please, Mama, I'm…I'm so scared…"

(I WILL TAKE YOU TO THE CITY)

(YOU WILL SWIM IN ITS DEPTHS)

(YOU WILL EMBRACE THE LIVING GOD)

The water was up to her throat now.

She looked into the eyes, smiling now. Then the smile faded. "I've…I've been diving for most of my life and now…now I realize what I'm afraid of…"

Drowning.

That's what her true fear had always been but she had not known it until now. She swallowed. The fear rose up inside her, black and enveloping.

"I don't want…to…drown…"

(YOU WENT DOWN THE RABBIT HOLE, ALICE, AND NOW THE CITY WILL RISE AND YOU'LL RISE WITH IT…)

Tears splashed from her eyes. The eyes of the beast blinked several times. It knew. It understood. Its eyes were the eyes of a mother that loved her and would deliver her gently and lovingly to her destiny, the ancestral heritage of her family who gathered in the green, sparkling depths at the end of their lives and were reborn, remade, to swim in the secret, sunken temples of Dagon, the one true god.

Tentacles covered her, shut out the world and there was only the cradle of their warmth and softness, their morphic splendor.

I'm ready, oh Mama, I'm ready now…

Javonivic went limp and closed her eyes, dreaming now. Beyond pain. And only when her mind had slipped entirely away did the tentacles begin to squeeze and exert dangerous pressure. The beast pulled her into itself, coveting her. Then its bulk slipped back down into the moon pool and out into the lake beneath.

The Entry Lock was filled with water.

The lights blinked out one after the other. Those in Main Lock followed suit.

And at the bottom of Lake Vordog there was an unbroken darkness.

And a serenity as Javy returned to the sea.

38
THE MONSTER

O rr saw it happen and he did not believe it.

Beneath the dark, boiling waters of the lake, he saw lights surfacing. Some tiny sliver of hope in him thought it might be the submersible coming up with his divers. A feeling of pure joy leaped inside him, but it was quickly extinguished when he saw that it was one of the Exosuits. The helmet broke the surface in an eruption of bubbles.

One of them survived! One of the divers survived!

In his mind, a simple plan evolved: he would use one of the winches and bring the suit aboard and get the diver out.

Then behind him, Anderson said, "We're going to die. It's come to kill us."

Which was an absolutely irrational thing to say. Orr was about to swear at him, chastise him for such stupid thinking. He even opened his mouth to do so, to vent the frustration and anger he felt…then, he watched the impossible happen. One of the suit arms reached from the water, its triple-pronged robotic manipulator grasped the deck railing like the talons of a beast and began to pull the suit up out of the water.

It could not be.

The Exosuits weighed well over a thousand pounds. No human being could have possibly made one do what it was now doing: crawling up onto the deck. The suit pulled itself up and then it did something even more fantastic—it stood. It was huge and deadly-looking, a robot from a sci-fi flick, water running from it and steam rising from it in plumes.

No man or woman would have been strong enough to hold that bulbous suit of armor upright. It would have taken titanic strength. If it wasn't for the buoyancy of water, it would have sank like a brick in the lake.

But, yet, it stood.

It was like a gigantic golem from an old movie, a perfect and primeval engine of destruction. Orr could feel the terrible menace coming from it. The helmet bubble was dark and he could not see inside it, yet the ID tag on it assured him that it was Bell's suit.

"Bell," he said. "Bell? Can you hear me?"

The hand pod reached out to him, rotary joints hissing, the triple prong manipulator clicking open and closed. It was strong enough to easily crush his arm. One blow from it could have cracked his skull like a walnut. The other hand pod was fitted with an industrial rotary saw with a twelve-inch titanium carbide blade that was used for deep-sea repair work. It could go through steel like cheese. It began to spin with a whirring noise.

"Anderson," Orr said in a low voice. "Get inside. Do you hear me? Get the fuck inside…"

He obeyed, jumping to his feet and running into the main deck house of the LSB.

The suit stepped forward with a Frankensteinian tread, the footpads thumping on the deck with seismic force. For so many years, Orr had looked on the hardsuits as absolute marvels of technology, he had never even thought of the monstrous things they could be if they were turned against you. Their aluminum anodized shells were nearly indestructible. It would have taken a .50-caliber round to breach them. The hydraulic and pneumatic systems were designed to function under intense undersea pressure, but out of the water, their destructive power was unbelievable. The triple-pronged manipulator—which looked very much like the claw of a bird of prey—could exert something like 10,000 pounds per square inch.

There was no getting around it: Anderson and he were in terrible danger. The Exosuit, possessed by some unnatural, alien force, had become a metallic predator that could have given The Terminator and Gort a run for their money.

Move carefully. It may be able to move quickly despite its bulk.

He backed slowly away as the suit approached him. There were halogen pods on either side of the acrylic bubble and now they were activated. The light exploded in Orr's face, their brilliance blinding him. He stumbled backwards, unable to see, fumbling over the deck and finally reaching the door. He pulled it open and slammed it shut, sealing it from the inside.

Outside, the suit thumped ever forward.

It was coming and he rather doubted anything could conceivably stop it.

"Sir…sir, it's right outside," Anderson managed, beads of sweat rolling down his face which was shriveled tight to the skull beneath with abject terror.

Orr tried to think. They needed a weapon, but he couldn't think of a dang thing. They had no guns. Firearms were forbidden in Antarctica by international law, despite what many silly, inaccurate movies led people to believe. There was plenty of iron around to be used as clubs and a welding unit in the maintenance shack on the forward deck…but both would require getting hazardously close to the suit and its deadly implements.

Boom.

The suit was banging on the door now. Each time its manipulator thudded against the stainless steel hatch, Anderson cried out like a horror-stricken child. He was a civilian and would be pretty much useless in the game of life and death that was coming.

Boom, boom, boom.

The door was shaking in its frame. It groaned with metal fatigue, its plates collapsing, screws ejected. Anderson was crying and blubbering, wrapping his arms around himself, nearly hysterical with fright.

"Goddammit, boy! Don't fold up on me now!" Orr shouted at him.

The door was hit again and this time it broke free of its frame. One of the hinges shot past Anderson with such force it threw blue sparks when it struck the deck plating; something Orr did not see because one of the plates bashed into him and threw him down.

The Exosuit smashed through the doorway, widening it to fit its girth.

One of the halogen pods on the helmet was torn off, the other strobing now with flickering, disorienting flashes of blue-white light.

Orr scrambled across the deck as the heavy tread of the suit made everything shake. It knocked a computer terminal out of the way and smashed a desk in two, crushing a small toolbox beneath its tread. Orr was in pain. He could barely straighten up. The door plate had bashed into him like a battering ram. He managed to get to his knees, wincing, white foam at his mouth from the exertion.

If you have internal injuries or a broken disc, you're finished, a voice said in his head.

But geared to survival, he would not listen. He could not give up. He could not give in. As the Exosuit destroyed everything in its path, he cried out, "ANDERSON! GET THE HELL OUT OF HERE! DO YOU HEAR ME? GET THE HELL OUT!"

The Exosuit marched ever forward, *thump, thump, thump.* It's claw manipulator shattered peripherals and gauges and screens. It reached up and tore a fresh air duct down, severing a steam pipe, and ripping free a power line that hit the deck sparking and smoking, throwing out a six-inch tongue of flame before its breakers cut the juice.

The deck house was plunged into darkness.

The only light came from the red EXIT sign over the rear door, the emergency deck lights shining dimly through the ports, and the ever-present strobing of the suit's halogens which made everything jump with shadows and jerky, surreal illumination. Its beams were filled with smoke and mist.

As Orr hobbled drunkenly toward the rear exit, he called out to Anderson again. The kid became confused in the flashing lights. He started in Orr's direction, fell over a chair, got to his feet and rammed right into a footlocker, which put him on his ass again. Then, despite Orr's shouts, he cut away and ducked through the archway across the room that led to the sleeping quarters.

"No! You fucking idiot, you're bottling yourself up!"

But Anderson did not hear him. The Exosuit advanced, then it turned, following Anderson. It bashed through the archway, tearing the metal trim free. Anderson began to scream, but there wasn't a damn thing Orr could do to help him. The deckhouse shook and creaked, the suit smashing through bulkheads and tearing doors from hinges.

Orr went through the rear exit and out onto the deck. He moved aft, trying to come up with a plan, anything. The cable car would be here in a matter of minutes and if that damn suit was still on the rampage, it would destroy it and nobody would ever leave.

Think! For the love of God, use your fucking brain!

As he hobbled his way aft, his back filled with white spikes of agony, he saw one of the portholes on the deckhouse get thrown open. And there came Anderson—shrieking, squealing, half out of his mind—but he squirmed through the port. He was a skinny little guy that probably barely weighed 130. He twisted and eeled his way out, falling to the deck as the Exosuit smashed into the cabin behind him.

He's going to make it, Orr thought, leaning up now against the shaking wall of a toolshed. *He's really going to make it.*

The outer bulkhead behind Anderson was hit with immense force, a huge bulge appearing in the sheet metal. Another appeared as it was rammed again. Anderson wriggled across the deck. There was a screeching, ear-splitting noise behind him as the Exosuit's industrial saw bit into the metal wall. It cut right through it, throwing a fountain of orange sparks and fiery ejecta. Then the bulkhead came apart, crashing to the deck and the Exosuit crashed through.

Anderson made a high-pitched wailing sound, jumping to his feet and running full out. He made it less than five feet before he smashed into the metal housing of a backup compressor. He hit it full on, foolishly looking behind him, and the impact tossed him back three, if not four, feet.

Orr, grimacing with pain, cried out, *"Get the hell out of there! Anderson, move!"*

He did, but far too late.

He got to his feet, but awkwardly from the impact. His reflexes were slow. He moved like a stunned cow. And just as he made to vault away, the Exosuit was on him. *Thump-thump-THUMP,* went its pounding footpads. The claw manipulator seized him by the shoulder and Orr clearly heard the mangling of flesh and the wet crunching of shattered bone. Even with Anderson's manic, insane shrieking, he heard it quite well. The manipulator lifted him up into the air, ever-tightening its grip, scissoring through meat, its prongs sinking deep into his scapula. Blood gushed and sprayed in wild loops, splattering against the mangled bulkhead and splashing against the gleaming shell of the Exosuit.

There was nothing Orr could do.

Even if some devastating weapon were at hand, he doubted he would have had the strength to wield it. Backlit by the emergency deck lights, mist and smoke swirling in the strobing halogens, the gigantic suit looked like an alien robot, an invader from a distant star, Anderson dangling in its grip like a prized specimen.

What happened then was inevitable.

The rotary saw came up with a hissing and clicking of hydraulics. The blade began to spin with that same insectile whirring like millions of pissed-off hornets. It grew so loud as it was powered to full that Orr had to cover his ears against the hypersonic screeching of it. As Anderson writhed in the grip of the manipulator, the saw came down, ripping into his scalp with an eruption of gore and bone chips, cutting through his skull and splitting his brain in half. The blade split his face like an oak plank and continued right down through his neck and torso until he was quite literally cut in half. Blood and macerated tissue and bone fragments sprayed through the air, gathering in a red-tinted nimbus over the Exosuit, a cloudburst of gore that spattered even Orr with hot droplets like a summer squall.

The remains of Anderson hit the deck with a wet splat. Then the suit's acrylic helmet bubble rotated in Orr's direction. Whatever energized the suit and glorified in sadism, had not forgotten about him.

Swaying side to side, the Exosuit advanced on him. Blood dripped from its shell, ran like tears down its view bubble, and streamed from the huge rebreather unit on its back.

Thump, thump, thump.

It was closing in on him.

It was going to kill him and, in his present shape, there wasn't a damn thing he could do about it. He was going to die here, in this place, on the deck of the LSB beneath the glacier, far below the grim white cemetery of Antarctica. He could barely move now as his injured back swelled unmercifully. Had he been in better shape, he might have made it to one of the engineering floats where he could have cooked the Exosuit and its occupant with one of the acetylene torches. He might have even made it into the submersible.

He leaned there against the toolshed, out of strength, out of fight. He was a dead man.

Wait…maybe he wasn't.

There was one chance, one extremely thin chance. As the Exosuit advanced on him, he hobbled his way around the deckhouse. It followed, never tiring, never hesitating. He had to put on the speed, but that was nearly impossible. Wracked with pain that made him feel dizzy and nauseous, he guided himself by the deck lights to the great winch on the aft deck that they used to lower and retrieve the ROV. He pushed and pushed himself beyond the limits of his endurance, but he made it.

Behind him, the Exosuit advanced, *thump, thump, thump.*

He would have one chance. Just the one chance.

Gritting his teeth, he climbed up into the operator's seat. He keyed the winch into life. It was dead. Power was cut. *Dammit.* He activated the backup and it started up.

The Exosuit kept coming, blood-stained manipulator opening and closing, the saw revving. Now it was a matter of how smart what possessed the suit was. If it was intelligent, there were many ways to avoid what he was going to do. If not…

It kept coming, its thundering footpads making the decks shake. Using the toggle control, Orr moved the winch arm into place. At the end of its cable was a massive clamp that could easily lift up to 5,000 pounds. He opened it and waited.

The Exosuit stopped, as if its occupant was considering the situation. Its strobing lights flashed on and off. Orr had to shield his eyes from them.

C'mon, you sonofabitch, he thought. *I'm right here.*

The helmet turned to the left, then the right as if searching for him. Maybe it had lost him behind the steel mesh operator's cage.

"BELL!" he shouted. "I'M OVER HERE!"

The helmet swung in his direction. The suit began to move. It thumped its way ever forward. No, it was not smart. It was a predator, a monster, a murdering beast that saw only his death. It moved closer and closer.

Though Orr should have been shivering down beneath the glacier, he was sweating. His eyes were wide, his mouth trembling as he waited for the Exosuit to get within range. What he was about to do was like playing one of those claw games at the fair, except what he hoped to catch was not a stuffed Mario or a Minion.

The Exosuit got closer.

His hand shook on the toggle.

It was bearing down.

Five feet.

Four.

Three.

Two.

One.

He turned on the winch spots and stopped the Exosuit momentarily with an explosion of brilliance. He dropped the clamp. It fell right on the suit and he closed it just as quick. The Exosuit flailed its arms, making hissing and popping and clicking noises. Orr, grinning now, activated the toggle and the winch lifted the suit five feet in the air where it dangled helplessly. It kept trying to cut itself free with the saw, but its aim was too far off.

Orr saw lights coming from above.

The cable car.

As it descended, it looked like a spacecraft from a movie, lighting up everything below it. It dropped finally all the way into its cradle and he made his way over there, climbing into the car. As he got into it, he saw the acrylic bubble of the Exosuit shatter and long, white, coiling tendrils emerge.

ESCAPE

The cable car was rising.

Inside the cage, Orr clung to the handrails. He was shaking, beyond tense, maybe close to a complete nervous breakdown. Below, he could see the decks of the LSB. The equipment. The buoy. The umbilical that reached down from the drill tower high above. All that ultra-expensive technology on the surface of the lake and on the bottom, abandoned now. As were the divers themselves.

Jesus.

The lights from the car illuminated the LSB as he was pulled up slowly away from it. He was nearly a hundred feet up now, the borehole through the icecap far above him yet. There was an arched ice-dome over the lake that was half a mile above its surface. It seemed like it would take years to get even that far, let alone through the borehole itself which ran for something like a mile through the glacier up to the drill tower above. The journey would take roughly an hour. And Orr knew it would be the longest hour of his life.

There wasn't much to be thankful for.

His divers were dead now, somewhere beneath the lake. The memory of them pained him a great deal because they meant a lot more to him than nameless casualty figures in an aborted operation. But the mission protocol was quite specific in every way: if contact was lost with the divers for forty-eight hours, they were not to go down after them, they were to abandon the LSB and return to the surface. It was all quite explicit.

Yet, there was guilt.

Orr knew they were all dead; he could feel it in his stomach like something he could not digest. Yet, the idea of not descending in a search-and-rescue op made him bleed inside. What if one of them, maybe, was still down there?

Stow it, he told himself. *You know the risks and you know the rules. So did they. It's over with. Mission scrubbed. And that's it. That's all there is to it.*

Yes, that's all there was to it. The mission was a failure. Four top-notch DSU divers were dead. A billion-dollars worth of equipment was abandoned. That's it. Orr felt the guilt, but he felt more than that. He was thankful that the automated winch/cable car system was still operational. That was something.

But what waited up there?

It wasn't only the Neptune and divers that had fallen silent for forty-eight hours now, but the drill team above.

The LSB was shrinking away into the shadows beneath the car, but it wasn't shrinking away fast enough to hide what was happening down there from his eyes. Orr looked down, his belly tightening, his nerves ringing out like the strings of a plucked lute.

He saw not only the Exosuit swinging back and forth from the clamp like a toy…but the bogies.

They were everywhere. Some were on the deck of the LSB, others perched on the cabin superstructure and the buoy tower itself. Still others were rising from the lake, fanning out their wings, droning and circling like moths.

Then the LSB was swallowed by the blackness.

But in the echoing void of the ice-dome, he could still hear them down there, buzzing and trilling. Smell that stench of ammonium that always heralded their presence.

"This damn thing go any faster?" he said under his breath.

But he knew it didn't. It was rising as fast as the winch was programmed to operate, within acceptable safety margins. No, the car was rising and it would reach the drill tower eventually. He just hoped there would be people up there when it did.

For below, the sound of those buzzing wings was getting louder.

40
REGRESSION

She was released.

She was free.

After a tedious, troubling life of bondage, Javy had finally morphed from a squirming larva to a beautiful butterfly. She had become an independent, free-roaming entity, yet she was part of the greater universal whole, a single energetic atom in a being of endless, godlike potential. All her life she had been shackled and caged, imprisoned by the onerous limitations of a terrestrial mammal, and now finally, ultimately, she was liberated and with liberation came deliverance from fear, paranoia, ego, jealousy, frustration, insecurity…in fact, all the petty, confining, self-defeating mechanisms of humankind.

The sea had called to her all her life.

And now, here in this place at the bottom of the ancient lake, she had answered the summons. She had slid down the rabbit hole like Alice and discovered a wonderful new reality.

I am here. I am now. I have always been.

Her genetic inheritance was her godhood and her purpose. She would make sacrifice at its cloven, webbed feet and be made one with it as it had been countless millennia before and would be again.

In the labyrinthine depths of the great sunken city, the leviathan had taken her. Here, she had shed her skin, releasing the beautiful, primordial organism within. It was like breathing for the first time. There was no anxiety in this place, only serenity because the grand, primeval blueprint for planet Earth was made known to her and she understood her place in it.

Those creatures that men and women feared with hysterical terror accepted her. They had been known by many names—Old Ones, Elder Things, Crinoids, and countless other meaningless titles. *Bogies. Yes, I remember they were called bogies.* But they were the engineers, the makers and creators, the cosmic farmers of the helix. They made the city as they had made all life on Earth and developed a simple intelligence in Pliocene apes that led to mankind, who were their crops, their sheep, a race that existed to be harvested, drained dry like a global battery.

The time was near.

Then she would call out in a siren's voice to her brothers and sisters that hid amongst the secret, sunken reefs and dwelled in the ruins of their abyssal crystalline cities. And, together, they would call forth and worship Father Dagon and Mother Hydra. Great Cthulhu would rise from his sunken tomb on R'yleh as the Dark Messenger had prophesied and Yog-Sothoth would throw open the gates and the songs of the King in Yellow would be heard once again.

Knowing these things, content that the time of her spawning was nearing, she swam through the cyclopean maze of the city, through tunnels and tangled passageways until she found the hidden birth-chamber of Leviathan.

I am here, Mother. I am here.

Rising high above her on a weedy nest of kelp, flowing luminescent mosses, and morbid, slithering marine growths, was the progenitor she had once called *Regina,* but was in truth a massive, squirming bathypelagic horror, a pulsating gelatinous monstrosity that looked down upon her with eyes of green quartz. Her spiny fins quivered, fleshy suckers pulsing, gills vibrating, and fungous-white tentacles undulating. She brooded upon a mountain of throbbing, gelid eggs as Javy herself would one blessed day.

(NOW THAT YOU HAVE BECOME THE LIVING GOD AWAITS YOU)

Yes, oh yes, oh yes…

(AND WE SHALL DWELL IN HIS HOUSE FOREVERMORE)

(PREPARE TO MAKE PRAISE)
(OFFER THY SPREAD LOINS BEFORE HIM)

Javy could feel his nearness.

She could feel the very life of the city. It was thrumming with vitality now that the living god had come through the gateway. It beat like a great heart as it woke up, its blood flowing, cells dividing, and neurons firing, a mammoth biomechanical organism which would now rise to the surface and release the living, hungry god.

41

ALONE

The cable car climbed and climbed through the borehole cut from the ancient glacial ice and the minutes dragged by like eternities.

Finally, Orr saw the drill tower above and he pressed his face to the window of the car and watched the light at the end of the tunnel. It occurred to him, as he watched it getting closer and closer, that it was all like some perverse mockery of the birth experience—moving down the womb towards the light.

But he didn't even want to speculate what birth was going to reveal this time around.

You're going back to the world, you idiot. The real world. You have a purpose. One last purpose.

Then the cable car was pulled clear of the borehole and the winch swung it automatically over to the wooden staging platform some distance away. No one came running up to greet him. The entire drill tower structure was entirely black and silent.

Where the hell is the crew?

The lights he had seen from below were only the security lights that surrounded the borehole itself. The main generator was out. There was no doubt of that. Everything at Kharkov and the drill tower was automated, computer-controlled. If the main generator failed, the back-ups would kick in as they apparently had. Even the cable car winch was automated so you could operate it from the LSB in an emergency, as Orr had. The back-up generators could theoretically run by themselves all winter, even the fuel-fired boilers were self-governing, siphoning diesel from the main tanks as needed.

Yes, things would keep running…but what about the crew?

Where were they?

There was a crew of six techs that monitored the borehole, the drilling apparatus, and the LSB far below. Three more people operated the station itself. So where in the hell were they?

They're gone and you know it. What happened to the dive team below also happened above. They've been purged. All of them. Did you really think they'd still be alive after two days of radio silence?

The lights from the cable car windows threw squares of illumination upon the wet floor of the drill tower. Other than that, there was only the glow of the borehole perimeter lights and a red EXIT sign in the distance.

Orr grabbed a flashlight from the emergency box at his feet. Then, breathing deeply, clenching his jaw against the pain of his injured back, he popped the latch and stepped out of the cable car.

His legs were shaky, muscles bunched up from the long ride, his back unbearably stiff. He panned the darkness with his flashlight. The heat was still on so it was warm. But that was about the only comfort. His footsteps on the wooden platform echoed out solemnly throughout the vast hollows of the drill tower. Something which heightened the deserted, claustrophobic feel of the place which was already in nightmarish overdrive.

Nerves, just nerves.

As he stood there, he realized he was having a bit of trouble breathing. Again, maybe it was nerves. But he didn't believe that for there was something damnably strange about the air…it didn't feel right. He likened it to being in a decompression chamber after a deep-saturation dive, the atmospheric pressure slowly being reduced to normal. This was very much like that. Right before they let you out, before pressure normalized, you could feel the weight of the air exerted upon you, the heaviness of it. And that's exactly how the air in the drill tower felt.

Not only heavy, but busy, agitated, crawling with energy. As if proof of that, a headache began to throb in the back of his skull.

He moved forward, slowly, painfully. His back felt like old plaster that would crack open at any moment. He wondered what would be worse: finding corpses or finding none at all? Knowing that everyone was dead and that he was alone or not knowing what had happened or what might happen next?

He really wasn't sure.

And, ultimately, does it even fucking matter now?

But as he panned about with his light, his brain filled with the horrible imagery he had known below—the Old One he had encountered on deck, the way it had leered at him; the images that Bell and Murphy had sent back of that town in the depths of the city, the ghosts haunting it; his own dreams aboard the LSB of that nameless city which looked very much like the elaborate, intertwined skeletons of deep-sea hydroid colonies he had seen as a young Navy diver, rising into the murk, so alien, so otherworldly—

Enough. Move. Continue mission.

He stepped away from the platform, not entirely sure what he might be stepping into, only that he could feel it. It thrummed around him like there was something wrong with the atoms in the air. He could feel minute pulsations of force crawling up and down his spine. His light beam danced about, picking out tool cribs, compressors, hoses and electrical lines, hoists, the gigantic drill itself which dangled high above like a cruise missile ready to fall. He kept going, moving around the great iron tripod of the drill. His light glanced off the housings of pumps and circulator tanks. Shadows flowed and leaped.

"Shit!" he suddenly cried out, casting his light in every which direction with a badly shaking hand. As he moved, the air crackled around him with tiny bursts of blue light. It looked like two static-charged blankets violently pulled apart.

On the other side of the tanks, he met a wall of utter blackness. But at its edges, there was a faint bluish glow. He moved towards it. The wall itself was only a section of fiberglass shielding from the drill apparatus used to contain ice chips and slush that cycled about when the hot water drill began melting through the glacier. His nerves feeling electrified, Orr maneuvered around the shielding and then the glow was right in front of him…and what it came from.

He let out a small, economical cry.

He froze up, a wild and gibbering terror rushing through him. He saw several cadaverous figures drifting in his direction, all of them limned in that blue, unreal electricity.

PRENATAL

ar, far below in the black, nightmare depths of the city, the living god was breathing. It was taking form and shape and substance.

Although it was incorporeal by nature and only a fragment of it was visible in the third dimension, it was alive and organic, throbbing and pulsing, cells dividing and tissues expanding, an embryonic horror that was coming to term.

Ready to be born in the dark womb of the city.

PRELUDE

They were dead.

They were all dead.

About fifteen feet away from Orr were six bodies…and they were all floating about ten feet off the floor. There was no menace in them as he'd first thought. They were simply dead. The techs. No wires or ropes held them. They floated of their own accord.

Like ghosts, he thought.

And they did look that way.

The bluish energy gave them a stark, ashen hue. Two of them floated face-up, arms and legs dangling limply, as if they were balanced precariously upon something. Another was standing straight up, head cocked to his shoulder. The others floated with arms and legs splayed like they'd been dropped from a great height. All of them were gradually drifting and Orr realized it was probably because he had disturbed the ether that held the corpses in stasis, sent ripples running through it. He couldn't say what that might be, only that it was some sort of energized field that apparently canceled out gravity.

Antigravity. That's what it was. The dream of physicists and engineers everywhere. He thrust his hand into the flow and yanked it back with a gasp. It was ice-cold.

The bodies drifted about. Though they were subtly lit by that energy,

Orr played his light over them. Whatever had happened, it had been a violent, ugly death for each of them. Their hands were hooked into claws, backs arched, faces contorted into screams. Ribbons of tangled blood that looked absolutely black hung from their mouths, puddling above them like pools of mist. Their eyes had been literally blown from their sockets and oozed in the air in clotted streamers of transparent tissue like squashed jellyfish. They were only connected to the hollowed orbits by threads of optic nerve. There were droplets of slime and blood floating everywhere. They looked like BBs. It was ghastly.

The antigravity stasis field intrigued him.

By all the laws of physics it was impossible, yet he was seeing it. He dug around in the pocket of his parka, found a couple coins. He chose a quarter and flipped it into the field. It arced up and started to fall as any object would and then…it just stopped, vibrating in mid-air, spinning end over end, bouncing off the foot of the nearest corpse and glancing off another and shearing through one of those suspended puddles of blood. The intrusion of a foreign body made the blood dissipate into a cloud of tiny, spreading bubbles.

That was enough.

He had to get on the radio.

He hobbled back around the shielding. He could see the red EXIT sign on the other side of the building. He started towards it. Somewhere above him, there was a noise. A *Ssshush-ssshush-ssshush* sort of noise. A whirring sound. The headache in his skull increased. His stomach rolled with nausea. And that was because of the sudden intrusion of a biting, pungent odor like hides treated with acidic chemicals. He only knew of one thing that smelled like that. And it was getting stronger…formaldehyde and ammonia.

They were here, now, in the darkness with him.

The bogies.

He knew it. He had smelled that horror on the deck of the LSB and nothing in his experience carried an odor like that. Like rancid leather, salted and stewed in harsh preservatives. It was enough to make your eyes water. He could feel the panic welling in him, overloading him with fright.

It's time. Enter the codes. Do your job.

He'd seen enough by then to accept the grim truth of what was going on in the tower. Yet, he hesitated. And he wondered if that wasn't because something inside him, some vestigial race memory perhaps, was reacting to what he was smelling, feeling, and sensing. Knowing it to be the most insidious horror his kind had ever known.

As he walked, Orr could feel cold and slinking things worrying at the edges of his thoughts. He shut them out. He had to. Around him, several luminous figures like huge moths darted about. Appearing. Disappearing. Amorphous, alien shapes, incorporeal, but not truly dead. But it was not just ghosts. Because there were other things now, stinking and slithering, physical evils that could not be denied. He could hear them whispering about in the dark, rustling like high cornstalks in a strong wind.

Wincing, he moved forward at a faster clip, ignoring the phantasms around him. He was shaking badly, oozing sweat that was hot and sour-smelling: the very briny juice of fear itself. A fluttering, semi-luminous figure swept past him and its aura was so cold that it froze the perspiration on his face. Low, buzzing sounds came from somewhere. A high, splintered trilling from somewhere else. He thought he saw a pod of globular red eyes just as moist as wet cherries winking out off to his left. Something whirred over his head and the stench of its passing made him want to scream.

Don't be afraid. You can't afford fear.

Yet, his heart was beating so hard it was like that of a terrified kitten.

I'm going to make it, he told himself. *I'm not going to be afraid of the terror by night or the pestilence that walks in darkness. Hell no. I'm gonna walk straight and proud like a man because I'm DSU and I'm going to follow my last orders right to the fucking grave. I am the vengeful hand of God that smites its enemies.*

He was within twenty feet of the exit when one of those damned things let go with a shrill piping cry. He went stiff as a post and screamed out every drop of terror in his soul. The drill tower began to echo with pipings and trillings, squeaks and chitterings. A constant *ree-ree-ree-ree* sound like millions of crickets singing out, amplified until it was deafening. Then a mad buzzing rose up as if from hundreds of wings. It was like the noise inside a bee apiary, except a thousand times louder.

Orr went down to his knees, covering his ears and then it simply passed and he could hear it outside the drill tower, filling the night. The bogies had abandoned the structure. He had no idea how they had gotten out. But maybe they had flown right through the walls like they were made of smoke.

Trying to catch his breath, he crawled painfully, stiffly over to the door and pulled it open.

Snow and cold blasted into his face. He saw the sky above. It was thick with heavy gray clouds and a buzzing black mass rose up into it like a swarm of hornets and vanished from sight.

He could see Kharkov Station. Targa House. The meteorology dome. The security lights marking its perimeter.

And the drill tower began to shake.

44

THE RISING

In fact, the entire world began to shake and tremble. Orr was thrown back inside the tower and the door slammed shut. He fought to his feet only to be dashed earthward again. Things were crashing and falling inside the tower. He could hear the creaking and groaning of metal fatigue. It was like the ice was being hit by an earthquake. He threw himself at the door and it flew open, tossing him aside. It came right off its hinges. He wedged himself in the doorway.

Kharkov Station buckled and heaved. A strange green light was coming from beneath the glacier. And the ice itself was cracking open, splitting asunder with jagged rents. Steam poured from it and it went to a slush that rolled and surged like molten lava. The drill tower was heaving and groaning, the ice popping and bubbling away. And from far below, that green phosphorescence was rising to the surface…a gigantic mass like some luminous sea creature breaching from the depths.

Orr saw Targa House sink into the bubbling sea.

He felt the heat of what was coming through the ice as steam and rivers of slush flowed through the doorway and he began to sink into it like an animal trapped in a tar pit. It was warm, unbelievably warm like bathwater. But it was sludgy and thick. He thrashed and fought. And what was coming from below continued to rise, burning and glowing like some molten reactor core rising from the frozen depths below and liquefying everything in its path.

You have one chance.
One little chance to end this.

He shambled back through the drill tower as it trembled around him, the great hot water drill swinging from side to side like a pendulum. Beams were falling, walls collapsing. Clouds of boiling steam blew up from the massive borehole itself. Although he was in terrible pain, he forced himself foreword. He didn't know exactly what was happening, but it was a bad omen. Something was being released down in the lake and he knew it would be a horror beyond imagination. He ducked beneath flying debris, stumbling, falling, crawling, inching his way until he got to the doorway of the command pod where all the technology of the drill system, the LSB below, and the Neptune habitat down in the lake was monitored and controlled. One of its windows shattered and shards of glass cut his face open.

The drill tower was burning.

He gagged on smoke and was scalded by hot steam, but he did not stop. In the pod, he activated the backup generator and all the screens, peripherals, and readouts lit up.

The code.
Enter the code.
Send it.

Yes, the very thing he had memorized from the classified folder in his safe on the LSB. The thing which had terrified him because his orders were most specific: if the operation failed and there was danger of contamination from the city itself, the doomsday scenario had to be activated. He logged himself onto the ONI's system, entering his security codes. It was online. There was still connectivity with the satellite above.

Do it.
Bring hell down upon you.

Swallowing, the drill tower literally coming down around him, he entered the final codes which would activate the device that was hidden in Kharkov Station. He had worried that it would be activated by the puppet masters of the Lake Vordog project, but in the end, his was the hand of God that initiated it.

The screen blinked red.

Ten minutes.
Ten fucking minutes.
Jesus.

45
BIRTH

Orr made it to the doorway of the tower and he knew he would never get any farther. He was out of fight. He would await the inevitable. Maybe the tower would collapse and crush him like an insect.

No matter.

No matter.

"Mission…complete," he muttered, shaking hip-deep in the slush which moved with sluggish waves and ripples.

The glacier was hissing and melting, boiling like a witch's cauldron, throwing out super-hot plumes of steam. The world contorted and quaked and that burning glow beneath the ice expanded, X-raying what was below, limning what was rising to the surface: *the city*. As the ice crackled and split, the structures of Kharkov Station either falling right over, flaring up like matchsticks, or exploding into kindling, the great city rose to the surface, making a beating sound like the constant booming of a battering ram. Its black, jagged towers and spires pierced the slush like fingers and the entire geometrically-profuse, skeletal mass broke through the glacier, rising, rising, seeming to tower hundreds of feet above. The world rumbled and shook with seismic vibrations, water and slush ejected high into the dark sky. The city oscillated with immense power, glowing a phosphorescent emerald, steaming and pulsating and then, as it seemed to fill the world for miles and miles, Kharkov Station split asunder and tossed aside, something even worse happened.

Something unthinkable.

Something horrendous.

Orr screamed at the sight of it.

The city was a gigantic shuddering womb, a gargantuan egg that shattered like an ice sculpture and out of it came a nightmare tide of oozing, placental, viscous slime that was smoldering and palpitating, a bubbling, gurgling fetal mutation that was born into this world, unfurling lashing fleshy umbilicals and snaking, webby feelers. Gigantic, glossy eyes opened with pink-orange pupils hundreds of feet across. It was a living, snotty birth that expanded and divided, foaming and slithering, a vermiform expulsion of noxious, alien flesh and writhing, cremating colors that filled Orr's brain with agonizing waves. It opened a thousand colossal, mewling, squealing mouths and—

And then there was a tremendous, earth-shattering roar as the tactical nuke waiting in the remains of Kharkov Station was ignited. There was a searing, blinding flash of light and the world went red and brilliant blue and luminous green as if the very auroras were drawn down from the heavens, igniting the ice itself which seemed to burn with a flickering, fissile illumination. The city and the thing born from it blazed and smoldered with a guttering incandescence like blazing magnesium and white phosphorus as a glowing, churning mushroom cloud rose up to the glittering stars above.

Then the shockwave wiped what was left of Kharkov Station right off the ice with screaming, irradiated winds that bore down with the strength of typhoons and tornadoes. Long before that happened, Orr was gone, melting down into the slush. The city was shattered into spoking, melting shards that sank back into the ice, freezing in state as the blaze flickered out, the cold and forever night of Antarctica rushing back in to fill the void.

Then there was only silence.

The howling winds.

And a darkness that went on forever.

GLOSSARY

ADS—Atmospheric Diving Suit

ATP—Active Thermal Probe

AUV—Autonomous Underwater Vehicle

DSSD—Diving System Support Detachment

DSSP—Deep Submergence Systems Project

DSU—Deep Submergence Unit

LSB—Life Support Buoy

NSF—National Science Foundation

ONI—Office of Naval Intelligence

ONR—Office of Naval Research

OSA—Official Secrets Act

SDV—Swimmer Delivery Vehicle

SPO—Special Projects Office

ABOUT THE AUTHOR

TIM CURRAN is the author of *Skin Medicine, Hive, Dead Sea, Resurrection, The Devil Next Door, Dead Sea Chronicles, Clownflesh,* and *Bad Girl in the Box*. His short stories have been collected in *Bone Marrow Stew* and *Zombie Pulp*. His novellas include "The Underdwelling," "The Corpse King," "Puppet Graveyard," and "Worm, and Blackout." His fiction has been translated into German, Japanese, Spanish, and Italian.

ABOUT THE ARTIST

Steeped in the enthralling fantasy and science-fiction illustrations of the 1960s, '70s, and '80s, artist and illustrator **K.L. TURNER** brings a bit of old-school painterly style to today's methods. With more than 30 years of experience in the arts, he expertly brings an expressionistic style into his illustrations to create compelling works which captivate and draw the viewer in. His works are found in media and galleries around the world, and celebrated in pop culture. A versatile creative type, Turner is also accomplished in the mediums of photography, sculpture, and the fine arts. Choosing to live and work on the beautiful front range of the Colorado Rocky Mountains where he was born and raised, he continues to derive inspiration from nature as well as cultural influences both at home and in his travels.

www.ingramcontent.com/pod-product-compliance
Lightning Source LLC
Chambersburg PA
CBHW030319020726
47493CB00004B/1081